Walter Scott

Caledonia

Walter Scott

Caledonia

ISBN/EAN: 9783337321574

Printed in Europe, USA, Canada, Australia, Japan

Cover: Foto ©Andreas Hilbeck / pixelio.de

More available books at **www.hansebooks.com**

CALEDONIA

DESCRIBED BY

SCOTT BURNS AND RAMSAY

With Illustrations by John Macwhirter

ENGRAVED BY K. PATERSON

WILLIAM P. NIMMO

LONDON AND EDINBURGH

1878

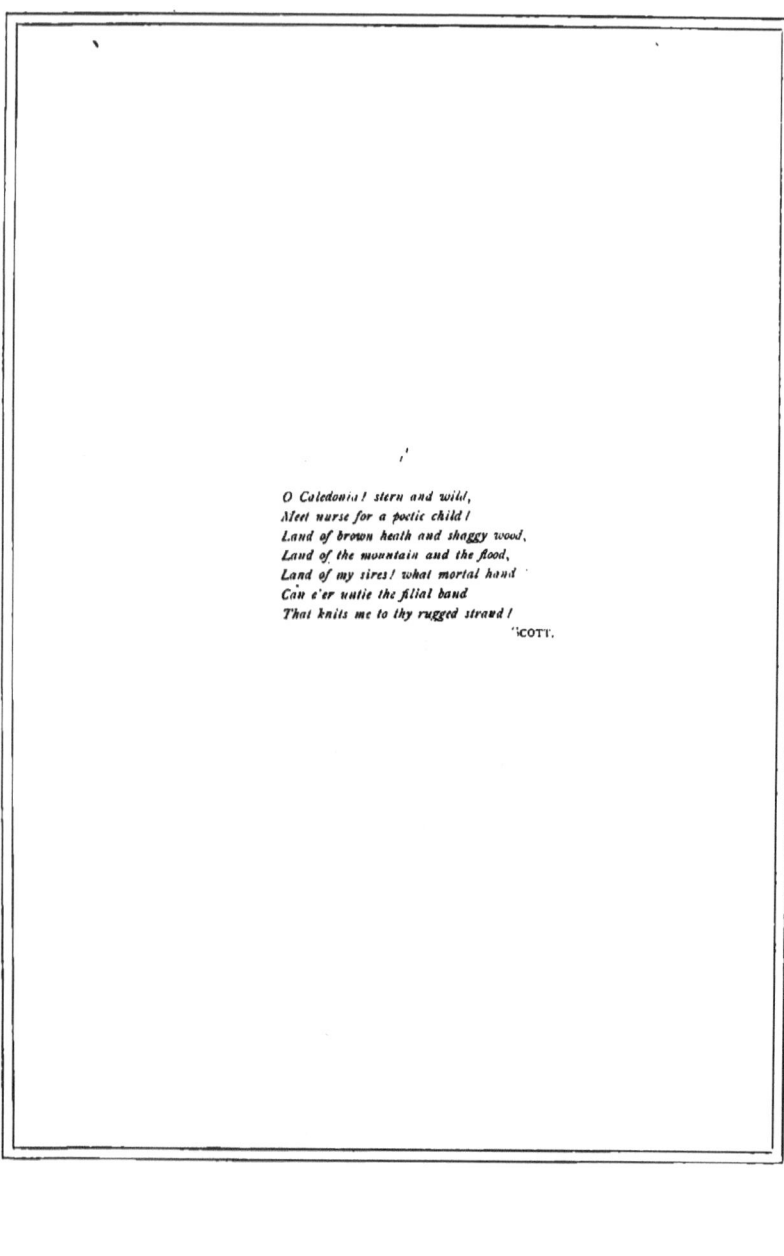

O Caledonia! stern and wild,
Meet nurse for a poetic child!
Land of brown heath and shaggy wood,
Land of the mountain and the flood,
Land of my sires! what mortal hand
Can e'er untie the filial band
That knits me to thy rugged strand!

SCOTT.

PREFACE.

HE I$_{LLUSTRATIONS}$ in this volume are solely
the work of the eminent Artist whose
name they bear. They have been drawn
from direct observation and from nature,
and they are intended as far as possible to illustrate the
more picturesque side of the landscape scenery of Scotland. The text will speak for itself. It has been selected
from the poetical works of three strongly national Poets
—Scott, Burns, and Ramsay. Whatever the distinct and
individual merits of these Poets may be, it may be said
of them, that they have all at least vied with each
other in describing the beauties and singing the glories
of their native land.

LIST OF ILLUSTRATIONS.

ENGRAVED BY R. PATERSON.

List of Illustrations.

CONTENTS.

Sir Walter Scott.

Robert Burns.

Contents.

SIR WALTER SCOTT

𝕾mailholm 𝕮ower.

—𝑜—

THEN rise those crags, that mountain tower,
Which charmed my fancy's wakening hour:
Though no broad river swept along,
To claim, perchance, heroic song;
Though sighed no groves in summer gale,
To prompt of love a softer tale;
Though scarce a puny streamlet's speed
Claimed homage from a shepherd's reed,

Smailholm Tower.

Yet was poetic impulse given,
By the green hill and clear blue heaven.
It was a barren scene, and wild,
Where naked cliffs were rudely piled ;
But ever and anon between
Lay velvet tufts of loveliest green ;
And well the lonely infant knew
Recesses where the wallflower grew,
And honeysuckle loved to crawl
Up the low crag and ruined wall.
I deemed such nooks the sweetest shade
The sun in all his round surveyed ;
And still I thought that shattered tower
The mightiest work of human power ;
And marvelled as the aged hind
With some strange tale bewitched my mind
Of forayers, who, with headlong force,
Down from that strength had spurred their horse,
Their southern rapine to renew,
Far in the distant Cheviots blue,
And, home returning, filled the hall
With revel, wassel-rout, and brawl.—
Methought that still with tramp and clang
The gateway's broken arches rang ;
Methought grim features, seamed with scars,
Glared through the windows' rusty bars.
And ever, by the winter hearth,
Old tales I heard of woe or mirth,

Smailholm Tower.

Of lovers' sleights, of ladies' charms,
Of witches' spells, of warriors' arms ;
Of patriot battles, won of old
By Wallace wight and Bruce the bold ;
Of later fields of feud and fight,
When, pouring from their Highland height,
The Scottish clans, in headlong sway,
Had swept the scarlet ranks away.
While stretched at length upon the floor,
Again I fought each combat o'er.
Pebbles and shells, in order laid,
The mimic ranks of war displayed ;
And onward still the Scottish Lion bore,
And still the scattered Southron fled before.

Introductory Epistle to Marmion.

SCENES FROM "MARMION."

——o——

Crichtoun Castle.

THAT castle rises on the steep
　Of the green vale of Tyne ;
And far beneath, where slow they creep
From pool to eddy, dark and deep,
Where alders moist, and willows weep,
　You hear her streams repine.
The towers in different ages rose ;
Their various architecture shows
　The builders' various hands ;
A mighty mass, that could oppose,
When deadliest hatred fired its foes,
　The vengeful Douglas bands.

Crichtoun ! though now thy miry court
　But pens the lazy steer and sheep,
　Thy turrets rude, and tottered Keep,
Have been the minstrel's loved resort.
Oft have I traced within thy fort,
　Of mouldering shields the mystic sense,
　Scutcheons of honour, or pretence,

Crichtoun Castle.

Quartered in old armorial sort,
  Remains of rude magnificence :
Nor wholly yet hath time defaced
  Thy lordly gallery fair ;
Nor yet the stony cord unbraced,
Whose twisted knots, with roses laced,
  Adorn thy ruined stair.
Still rises unimpaired, below,
The courtyard's graceful portico ;
Above its cornice, row and row
Of fair hewn facets richly show
  Their pointed diamond form,
Though there but houseless cattle go
  To shield them from the storm.
And, shuddering, still may we explore,
  Where oft whilome were captives pent,
The darkness of thy Massy More ;[1]
  Or, from thy grass-grown battlement,
May trace, in undulating line,
The sluggish mazes of the Tyne.

Another aspect Crichtoun showed,
As through its portal Marmion rode ;
But yet 'twas melancholy state
Received him at the outer gate ;

---

[1] The pit, or prison vault.

Crichtoun Castle.

For none were in the castle then,
But women, boys, or aged men.
With eyes scarce dried, the sorrowing dame,
To welcome noble Marmion came ;
Her son, a strippling twelve years old,
Proffered the Baron's rein to-hold ;
For each man, that could draw a sword,
Had marched that morning with their lord,
Earl Adam Hepburn—he who died
On Flodden, by his sovereign's side.
Long may his lady look in vain !
She ne'er shall see his gallant train
Come sweeping back through Crichtoun-Dean.
'Twas a brave race, before the name
Of hated Bothwell stained their fame.

And here two days did Marmion rest,
    With every rite that honour claims,
Attended as the King's own guest,—
    Such the command of royal James ;
Who marshalled then his land's array,
Upon the Borough moor that lay.
Perchance he would not foeman's eye
Upon his gathering host should pry,
Till full prepared was every band
To march against the English land.

Crichtoun Castle.

Here while they dwelt, did Lindesay's wit
Oft cheer the Baron's moodier fit ;
And, in his turn, he knew to prize
Lord Marmion's powerful mind and wise—
Trained in the lore of Rome and Greece,
And policies of war and peace.
It chanced, as fell the second night,
    That on the battlements they walked,
And, by the slowly fading light,
    Of varying topics talked ;
And, unaware, the Herald-bard
Said Marmion might his toil have spared,
    In travelling so far ;
For that a messenger from heaven
In vain to James had counsel given
    Against the English war :
And, closer questioned, thus he told
A tale, which chronicles of old
In Scottish story have enrolled :—

*" In Scotland, far beyond compare
Linlithgow is excelling."*

Sir David Lindesay's Tale.

———o———

" Of all the palaces so fair,
  Built for the royal dwelling,
In Scotland, far beyond compare
  Linlithgow is excelling;
And in its park, in jovial June,
How sweet the merry linnet's tune,

Sir David Lindesay's Tale.

How blithe the blackbird's lay!
The wild buck bells from ferny brake,
The coot dives merry on the lake,
The saddest heart might pleasure take
   To see all nature gay.
But June is to our Sovereign dear
The heaviest month in all the year:
Too well his cause of grief you know,—
June saw his father's overthrow.
Woe to the traitors, who could bring
The princely boy against his King!
Still in his conscience burns the sting.
In offices as strict as Lent,
King James's June is ever spent.

"When last this ruthful month was come,
And in Linlithgow's holy dome
   The King, as wont, was praying;
While for his royal father's soul
The chanters sung, the bells did toll,
   The Bishop mass was saying—
For now the year brought round again
The day the luckless king was slain—
   In Katharine's aisle the Monarch knelt,
   With sackcloth shirt, and iron belt,
      And eyes with sorrow streaming;

Sir David Lindesay's Tale.

Around him, in their stalls of state,
The Thistle's Knight-Companions sate,
   Their banners o'er them beaming.
I too was there, and, sooth to tell,
Bedeafened with the jangling knell,
Was watching where the sunbeams fell,
   Through the stained casement gleaming ;
But, while I marked what next befell,
   It seemed as I were dreaming.
Stepped from the crowd a ghostly wight,
In azure gown, with cincture white ;
His forehead bald, his head was bare,
Down hung at length his yellow hair.—
Now, mock me not, when, good my lord,
I pledge to you my knightly word,
That, when I saw his placid grace,
His simple majesty of face,
His solemn bearing, and his pace
   So stately gliding on ;
Seemed to me ne'er did limner paint
So just an image of the saint,
Who propped the Virgin in her faint,—
   The loved Apostle John.

" He stepped before the Monarch's chair,
And stood with rustic plainness there,
   And little reverence made ;

Sir David Lindesay's Tale.

Nor head, nor body, bowed nor bent,
But on the desk his arm he leant,
   And words like these he said,
In a low voice,—but never tone
So thrilled through vein, and nerve, and bone :—
  'My mother sent me from afar,
  Sir King, to warn thee not to war,—
    Woe waits on thine array ;
  If war thou wilt, of woman fair,
  Her witching wiles and wanton snare,
  James Stuart, doubly warned, beware :·
    God keep thee as He may !'—
The wondering Monarch seemed to seek
    For answer, and found none ;
And when he raised his head to speak,
    The monitor was gone.
The Marshal and myself had cast
To stop him as he outward passed ;
But, lighter than the whirlwind's blast,
    He vanished from our eyes,
Like sunbeam on the billow cast,
    That glances but, and dies."

While Lindesay told this marvel strange,
  The twilight was so pale,
He marked not Marmion's colour change,
  While listening to the tale :

But, after a suspended pause,
The Baron spoke :—" Of Nature's laws
  So strong I hold the force,
That never superhuman cause
  Could e'er control their course ;
And, three days since, had judged your aim
Was but to make your guest your game.
But I have seen, since past the Tweed,
What much has changed my sceptic creed,
And made me credit aught."—He stayed,
And seemed to wish his words unsaid ;
  But, by that strong emotion pressed,
  Which prompts us to unload our breast,
    Even when discovery's pain,
  To Lindesay did at length unfold
  The tale his village host had told,
    At Gifford, to his train.
Nought of the Palmer says he there,
And nought of Constance, or of Clare :
The thoughts, which broke his sleep, he seems
To mention but as feverish dreams.

" In vain," said he, " to rest I spread
My burning limbs, and couched my head,
  Fantastic thoughts returned ;
And, by their wild dominion led,
  My heart within me burned.

Sir David Lindesay's Tale.

So sore was the delirious goad,
I took my steed, and forth I rode,
And, as the moon shone bright and cold,
Soon reached the camp upon the wold.
The southern entrance I passed through,
And halted, and my bugle blew.
Methought an answer met my ear,—
Yet was the blast so low and drear,
So hollow, and so faintly blown,
It might be echo of my own.

" Thus judging, for a little space
I listened, ere I left the place;
    But scarce could trust my eyes,
Nor yet can think they served me true,
When sudden in the ring I view,
In form distinct of shape and hue,
    A mounted champion rise.—
I've fought, Lord-Lyon, many a day,
In single fight, and mixed affray,
And ever, I myself may say,
    Have borne me as a knight;
But when this unexpected foe
Seemed starting from the gulf below,—
I care not though the truth I show,—
    I trembled with affright;

Sir David Lindesay's Tale.

And as I placed in rest my spear,
My hand so shook for very fear,
  I scarce could couch it right.

"Why need my tongue the issue tell?
We ran our course,—my charger fell;—
What could he 'gainst the shock of hell?
  I rolled upon the plain.
High o'er my head, with threatening hand,
The spectre shook his naked brand,—
  Yet did the worst remain;
My dazzled eyes I upward cast,—
Not opening hell itself could blast
  Their sight, like what I saw!
Full on his face the moonbeam strook,—
A face could never be mistook!
I knew the stern vindictive look,
  And held my breath for awe.
I saw the face of one who, fled
To foreign climes, has long been dead.—
  I well believe the last;
For ne'er, from visor raised, did stare
A human warrior, with a glare
  So grimly and so ghast.
Thrice o'er my head he shook the blade;
. But when to good Saint George I prayed,

Sir David Lindesay's Tale.

(The first time e'er I asked his aid,)
  He plunged it in the sheath;
And, on his courser mounting light,
He seemed to vanish from my sight:
The moonbeam drooped, and deepest night
  Sunk down upon the heath.—
'Twere long to tell what cause I have
  To know his face, that met me there,
Called by his hatred from the grave,
  To cumber upper air:
Dead or alive, good cause had he
To be my mortal enemy."

Marvelled Sir David of the Mount;
Then, learned in story, 'gan recount
  Such chance had happed of old,
When once, near Norham, there did fight
A spectre fell, of fiendish might,
In likeness of a Scottish knight,
  With Brian Bulmer bold,
And trained him nigh to disallow
The aid of his baptismal vow.
"And such a phantom, too, 'tis said,
With Highland broadsword, targe, and plaid,
  And fingers red with gore,
Is seen in Rothiemurcus glade,
Or where the sable pine-trees shade

Sir David Lindesay's Tale.

Dark Tomantoul, and Achnaslaid,
   Dromouchty, or Glenmore.
And yet, whate'er such legends say,
Of warlike demon, ghost, or fay,
   On mountain, moor, or plain,
Spotless in faith, in bosom bold,
True son of chivalry should hold
   These midnight terrors vain :
For seldom have such spirits power
To harm, save in the evil hour,
When guilt we meditate within,
Or harbour unrepented sin."—
Lord Marmion turned him half aside,
And twice to clear his voice he tried,
   Then pressed Sir David's hand,—
But nought, at length, in answer said ;
And here their farther converse stayed,
   Each ordering that his band
Should bowne them with the rising day,
To Scotland's camp to take their way,—
   Such was the King's command.

Early they took Dun-Edin's road,
And I could trace each step they trode ;
Hill, brook, nor dell, nor rock, nor stone
Lies on the path to me unknown.
Much might it boast of storied lore ;

But, passing such digression o'er,
Suffice it, that their route was laid
Across the furzy hills of Braid.
They passed the glen and scanty rill,
And climbed the opposing bank, until
They gained the top of Blackford Hill.

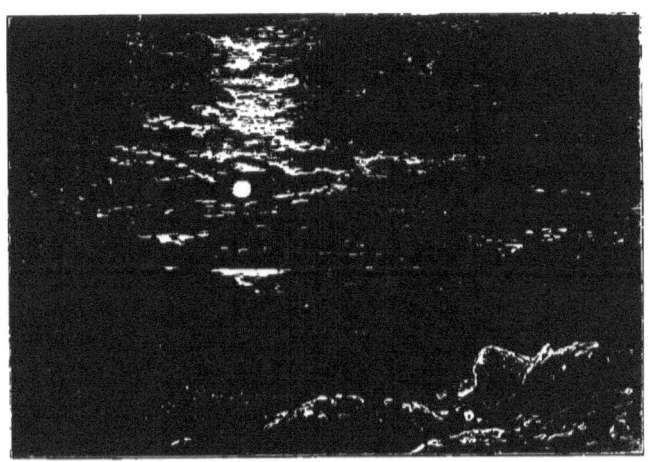

" Their route was laid
Across the furzy hills of Braid."

Blackford! on whose uncultured breast,
  Among the broom, the thorn, and whin,
A truant boy, I sought the nest,
Or listed, as I lay at rest,
  While rose, on breezes thin,

The Borough-Moor.

The murmur of the city crowd,
And, from his steeple jangling loud,
  Saint Giles's mingling din.
Now, from the summit to the plain,
Waves all the hill with yellow grain;
  And o'er the landscape as I look,
Nought do I see unchanged remain,
  Save the rude cliffs and chiming brook.
To me they make a heavy moan,
Of early friendships past and gone.

But different far the change has been,
  Since Marmion, from the crown
Of Blackford saw that martial scene
  Upon the bent so brown:
Thousand pavilions, white as snow,
Spread o'er the Borough-moor below,
  Upland, and dale, and down:—
A thousand did I say? I ween,
Thousands on thousands there were seen,
That chequered all the heath between
  The streamlet and the town;
In crossing ranks extending far,
Forming a camp irregular;
Oft giving way, where still there stood
Some reliques of the old oak-wood,

The Borough-Moor.

That darkly huge did intervene,
And tame the glaring white with green :
In these extended lines there lay
A martial kingdom's vast array.

For from Hebudes, dark with rain,
To eastern Lodon's fertile plain,
And from the southern Redswire edge,
To farthest Rosse's rocky ledge ;
From west to east, from south to north,
Scotland sent all her warriors forth.
Marmion might hear the mingled hum
Of myriads up the mountain come ;
The horses' tramp, and tingling clank,
Where chiefs reviewed their vassal rank,
    And charger's shrilling neigh ;
And see the shifting lines advance,
While frequent flashed, from shield and lance,
    The sun's reflected ray.

Thin curling in the morning air,
The wreaths of failing smoke declare,
To embers now the brands decayed,
Where the night-watch their fires had made.
They saw, slow rolling on the plain,
Full many a baggage-cart and wain,

The Royal Banner.

And dire artillery's clumsy car,
By sluggish oxen tugged to war;
And there were Borthwick's Sisters Seven,[1]
And culverins which France had given.
Ill-omened gift! the guns remain
The conqueror's spoil on Flodden plain.

Nor marked they less, where in the air
A thousand streamers flaunted fair;
    Various in shape, device, and hue,
    Green, sanguine, purple, red, and blue,
Broad, narrow, swallow-tailed, and square,
Scroll, pennon, pensil, bandrol,[2] there
    O'er the pavilions flew.
Highest, and midmost, was descried
The royal banner, floating wide;
    The staff, a pine-tree strong and straight,
        Pitched deeply in a massive stone,
        Which still in memory is shown,
    Yet bent beneath the standard's weight,
Whene'er the western wind unrolled,
With toil, the huge and cumbrous fold,
    And gave to view the dazzling field,
    Where, in proud Scotland's royal shield,
The ruddy Lion ramped in gold.

[1] Seven culverins so called, cast by one Borthwick.
[2] Each of these feudal ensigns intimated the different rank of those entitled to display them.

Marmion.

Lord Marmion viewed the landscape bright,—
He viewed it with a chief's delight,—
Until within him burned his heart,
And lightning from his eye did part,
   As on the battle-day ;
Such glance did falcon never dart,
   When stooping on his prey.
" Oh ! well, Lord-Lion, hast thou said,
Thy King from warfare to dissuade
   Were but a vain essay ;
For, by Saint George, were that host mine,
Not power infernal, nor divine,
Should once to peace my soul incline,
Till I had dimmed their armour's shine
   In glorious battle fray ! "—
Answered the bard, of milder mood :
" Fair is the sight,—and yet 'twere good,
   That kings would think withal,
When peace and wealth their land have blessed,
'Tis better to sit still at rest,
   Than rise, perchance to fall."

Still on the spot Lord Marmion stayed,
For fairer scene he ne'er surveyed.
   When sated with the martial show
   That peopled all the plain below,

Edinburgh.

The wandering eye could o'er it go,
And mark the distant city glow
  With gloomy splendour red ;
For on the smoke-wreaths, huge and slow,
That round her sable turrets flow,
  The morning beams were shed,
And tinged them with a lustre proud,
Like that which streaks a thunder-cloud.
Such dusky grandeur clothed the height,
Where the huge castle holds its state,
  And all the steep slope down,
Whose ridgy back heaves to the sky,
Piled deep and massy, close and high,
  Mine own romantic town !
But northward far, with purer blaze,
On Ochil mountains fell the rays,
And as each heathy top they kissed,
It gleamed a purple amethyst.
  Yonder the shores of Fife you saw ;
  Here Preston Bay, and Berwick Law ;
    And, broad between them rolled,
  The gallant Firth the eye might note,
  Whose islands on its bosom float,
    Like emeralds chased in gold.
Fitz-Eustace' heart felt closely pent ;
As if to give his rapture vent,
The spur he to his charger lent,
  And raised his bridle-hand,

And, making demi-volte in air,
Cried, "Where's the coward that would not dare
  To fight for such a land!"
The Lindesay smiled his joy to see;
Nor Marmion's frown repressed his glee.

Lady Heron's Song.

—o—

THE Queen sits lone in Lithgow pile,
 And weeps the weary day,
The war against her native soil,
Her Monarch's risk in battle broil;—
And in gay Holy-Rood, the while,
Dame Heron rises with a smile
 Upon the harp to play.
Fair was her rounded arm, as o'er
 The strings her fingers flew;
And as she touched, and tuned them all,
Even her bosom's rise and fall
 Was plainer given to view;
For, all for heat, was laid aside
Her wimple, and her hood untied.
And first she pitched her voice to sing,
Then glanced her dark eye on the King,
And then around the silent ring;
And laughed, and blushed, and oft did say
Her pretty oath, by Yea, and Nay,
She could not, would not, durst not play!

Lady Heron's Song.

At length, upon the harp, with glee,
Mingled with arch simplicity,
A soft, yet lively, air she rung,
While thus the wily lady sung.

Lochinvar.

O, young Lochinvar is come out of the west,
Through all the wide Border his steed was the best,
And save his good broadsword he weapons had none;
He rode all unarmed, and he rode all alone.
So faithful in love, and so dauntless in war,
There never was knight like the young Lochinvar.

He stayed not for brake, and he stopped not for stone,
He swam the Eske river where ford there was none;
But, ere he alighted at Netherby gate,
The bride had consented, the gallant came late:
For a laggard in love, and a dastard in war,
Was to wed the fair Ellen of brave Lochinvar.

So boldly he entered the Netherby hall,
Among bride's-men and kinsmen, and brothers and all:
Then spoke the bride's father, his hand on his sword,
(For the poor craven bridegroom said never a word,)
" O come ye in peace here, or come ye in war,
Or to dance at our bridal, young Lord Lochinvar?"

Lady Heron's Song.

" I long wooed your daughter, my suit you denied ;
Love swells like the Solway, but ebbs like its tide—
And now I am come, with this lost love of mine,
To lead but one measure, drink one cup of wine.
There are maidens in Scotland more lovely by far,
That would gladly be bride to the young Lochinvar."

The bride kissed the goblet ; the knight took it up,
He quaffed off the wine, and he threw down the cup,
She looked down to blush, and she looked up to sigh,
With a smile on her lips and a tear in her eye.
He took her soft hand, ere her mother could bar,—
" Now tread we a measure !" said young Lochinvar.

So stately his form, and so lovely her face,
That never a hall such a galliard did grace ;
While her mother did fret, and her father did fume,
And the bridegroom stood dangling his bonnet and plume ;
And the bride-maidens whispered, " 'Twere better by far
To have matched our fair cousin with young Lochinvar."

One touch to her hand, and one word in her ear,
When they reached the hall door and the charger stood near ;
So light to the croupe the fair lady he swung,
So light to the saddle before her he sprung !—
" She is won ! we are gone, over bank, bush, and scaur ;
They'll have fleet steeds that follow," quoth young Lochinvar.

Lady Heron's Song.

There was mounting 'mong Græmes of the Netherby clan ;
Forsters, Fenwicks, and Musgraves, they rode and they ran :
There was racing, and chasing, on Cannobie Lee,
But the lost bride of Netherby ne'er did they see.
So daring in love, and so dauntless in war,
Have ye e'er heard of gallant like young Lochinvar ?

The Monarch o'er the syren hung,
And beat the measure as she sung ;
And, pressing closer, and more near,
He whispered praises in her ear.
In loud applause the courtiers vied ;
And ladies winked and spoke aside.
The witching dame to Marmion threw
A glance, where seemed to reign
The pride that claims applauses due,
And of her royal conquest, too,
A real or feigned disdain :
Familiar was the look, and told,
Marmion and she were friends of old.
The King observed their meeting eyes,
With something like displeased surprise ;
For monarchs ill can rivals brook,
Even in a word, or smile, or look.
Straight took he forth the parchment broad,
Which Marmion's high commission showed :

Lady Heron's Song.

"Our Borders sacked by many a raid,
Our peaceful liegemen robbed," he said;
"On day of truce our Warden slain,
Stout Barton killed, his vassals ta'en—
Unworthy were we here to reign,
Should these for vengeance cry in vain;
Our full defiance, hate, and scorn,
Our herald has to Henry borne."

Cantallon Castle.

—o—

But scant three miles the band had rode,
  When o'er a height they passed,
And, sudden, close before them showed
  His towers, Tantallon vast:
Broad, massive, high, and stretching far,
And held impregnable in war.
On a projecting rock they rose,
And round three sides the ocean flows;
The fourth did battled walls enclose,
  And double mound and fosse.
By narrow drawbridge, outworks strong,
Through studded gates, an entrance long,
  To the main court they cross.
It was a wide and stately square;
Around were lodgings, fit and fair,
  And towers of various form,
Which on the court projected far,
And broke its lines quadrangular.
Here was square keep, there turret high,
Or pinnacle that sought the sky,
Whence oft the Warder could descry
  The gathering ocean storm.

✢   ✢   ✢   ✢   ✢

Tantallon Castle.

I said, Tantallon's dizzy steep
Hung o'er the margin of the deep.
Many a rude tower and rampart there
Repelled the insult of the air,
Which, when the tempest vexed the sky,
Half breeze, half spray, came whistling by.
Above the rest, a turret square
Did o'er its Gothic entrance bear,
Of sculpture rude, a stony shield;
The Bloody Heart was in the field,
And in the chief three mullets stood,
The cognizance of Douglas blood.
The turret held a narrow stair,
Which, mounted, gave you access where
A parapet's embattled row
Did seaward round the castle go;
Sometimes in dizzy steps descending,
Sometimes in narrow circuit bending,
Sometimes in platform broad extending,
Its varying circle did combine
Bulwark, and bartizan, and line,
And bastion, tower, and vantage-coign;
Above the booming ocean leant
The far-projecting battlement;
The billows burst, in ceaseless flow,
Upon the precipice below.
Where'er Tantallon faced the land,
Gate-works, and walls, were strongly manned;

" *Tantallon's dizzy steep*
Hung o'er the margin of the deep."

Cantallon Castle.

No need upon the sea-girt side ;
The steepy rock, and frantic tide,
Approach of human step denied ;
And thus these lines, and ramparts rude,
Were left in deepest solitude.

Flodden.

———◦———

THE Scots beheld the English host
Leave Barmore-wood, their evening post,
And heedful watched them as they crossed
The Till by Twisel bridge.
High sight it is, and haughty, while
They dive into the deep defile ;
Beneath the caverned cliff they fall,
Beneath the castle's airy wall.
By rock, by oak, by hawthorn-tree,
Troop after troop are disappearing ;
Troop after troop their banners rearing,
Upon the eastern bank you see.
Still pouring down the rocky den,
Where flows the sullen Till,
And rising from the dim-wood glen,
Standards on standards, men on men,
In slow succession still,
And sweeping o'er the Gothic arch,
And pressing on, in ceaseless march,
To gain the opposing hill.
That morn, to many a trumpet-clang,
Twisel ! thy rock's deep echo rang ;

Flodden.

And many a chief of birth and rank,
Saint Helen! at thy fountain drank.
Thy hawthorn glade, which now we see
In spring-tide bloom so lavishly,
Had then from many an axe its doom,
To give the marching columns room.

And why stands Scotland idly now,
Dark Flodden! on thy airy brow,
Since England gains the pass the while,
And struggles through the deep defile?
What checks the fiery soul of James?
Why sits that champion of the dames
　　Inactive on his steed,
And sees, between him and his land,
Between him and Tweed's southern strand,
　　His host Lord Surrey lead?
What 'vails the vain knight-errant's brand?—
O, Douglas, for thy leading wand!
　　Fierce Randolph, for thy speed!
O for one hour of Wallace wight,
Or well-skilled Bruce, to rule the fight,
And cry—"Saint Andrew and our right!"
Another sight had seen that morn,
From Fate's dark book a leaf been torn,
And Flodden had been Bannockburn!—

Flodden.

The precious hour had passed in vain,
And England's host has gained the plain ;
Wheeling their march, and circling still,
Around the base of Flodden hill.

Scenes from the "Lady of the Lake."

———◇———

THE stag at eve had drunk his fill,
Where danced the moon on Monan's rill,
And deep his midnight lair had made
In lone Glenartney's hazel shade;
But, when the sun his beacon red
Had kindled on Benvoirlich's head,
The deep-mouthed bloodhound's heavy bay
Resounded up the rocky way,

Lady of the Lake.

And faint, from farther distance borne,
Were heard the clanging hoof and horn.

As chief who hears his warder call,
" To arms! the foemen storm the wall,"—
The antlered monarch of the waste
Sprung from his heathery couch in haste.
But, ere his fleet career he took,
The dewdrops from his flanks he shook;
Like crested leader proud and high,
Tossed his beamed frontlet to the sky;
A moment gazed adown the dale,
A moment snuffed the tainted gale,
A moment listened to the cry,
That thickened as the chase drew nigh;
Then, as the headmost foes appeared,
With one brave bound the copse he cleared,
And stretching forward free and far,
Sought the wild heaths of Uam-Var.

Yelled on the view the opening pack,
Rock, glen, and cavern paid them back;
To many a mingled sound at once
The awakened mountain gave response.
A hundred dogs bayed deep and strong,
Clattered a hundred steeds along,

Lady of the Lake.

Their peal the merry horns rang out,
A hundred voices joined the shout;
With hark and whoop and wild halloo,
No rest Benvoirlich's echoes knew.
Far from the tumult fled the roe,
Close in her covert cowered the doe,
The falcon, from her cairn on high,
Cast on the rout a wondering eye,
Till far beyond her piercing ken
The hurricane had swept the glen.
Faint, and more faint, its failing din
Returned from cavern, cliff, and linn,
And silence settled, wide and still,
On the lone wood and mighty hill.

Less loud the sounds of sylvan war
Disturbed the heights of Uam-Var,
And roused the cavern, where, 'tis told,
A giant made his den of old;
For ere that steep ascent was won,
High in his pathway hung the sun,
And many a gallant, stayed perforce,
Was fain to breathe his faltering horse;
And of the trackers of the deer
Scarce half the lessening pack was near;
So shrewdly, on the mountain-side,
Had the bold burst their mettle tried.

Lady of the Lake.

The noble stag was pausing now
Upon the mountain's southern brow,
Where broad extended, far beneath,
The varied realms of fair Menteith.
With anxious eye he wandered o'er
Mountain and meadow, moss and moor,
And pondered refuge from his toil,
By far Lochard or Aberfoyle.
But nearer was the copse-wood grey,
That waved and wept on Loch Achray,
And mingled with the pine-trees blue
On the bold cliffs of Ben Venue.
Fresh vigour with the hope returned,
With flying foot the heath he spurned, ·
Held westward with unwearied race,
And left behind the panting chase.

'Twere long to tell what steeds gave o'er,
As swept the hunt through Cambus-more ;
What reins were tightened in despair,
When rose Benledi's ridge in air ;
Who flagged upon Bochastle's heath,
Who shunned to stem the flooded Teith,—
For twice, that day, from shore to shore,
The gallant stag swam stoutly o'er.
Few were the stragglers, following far,
That reached the lake of Vennachar ;

Lady of the Lake.

And when the Brigg of Turk was won,
The headmost horseman rode alone.

Alone, but with unbated zeal,
That horseman plied the scourge and steel;
For, jaded now, and spent with toil,
Embossed with foam, and dark with soil,
While every gasp with sobs he drew,
The labouring stag strained full in view.
Two dogs of black Saint Hubert's breed,
Unmatched for courage, breath, and speed,
Fast on his flying traces came,
And all but won that desperate game;
For, scarce a spear's length from his haunch,
Vindictive toiled the bloodhounds stanch;
Nor nearer might the dogs attain,
Nor farther might the quarry strain.
Thus up the margin of the lake,
Between the precipice and brake,
O'er stock and rock their race they take.

The Hunter marked that mountain high,
The lone lake's western boundary,
And deemed the stag must turn to bay,
Where that rude rampart barred the way;

Lady of the Lake.

Already glorying in the prize,
Measured his antlers with his eyes;
For the death-wound, and death halloo,
Mustered his breath, his whinyard drew;
But, thundering as he came prepared,
With ready arm and weapon bared,

" *In the deep Trosachs' wildest nook*
His solitary refuge took."

The wily quarry shunned the shock,
And turned him from the opposing rock;
Then, dashing down a darksome glen,
Soon lost to hound and hunter's ken.
In the deep Trosachs' wildest nook
His solitary refuge took.

Lady of the Lake.

There, while close couched, the thicket shed
Cold dews and wild flowers on his head,
He heard the baffled dogs in vain
Rave through the hollow pass amain,
Chiding the rocks that yelled again.

Close on the hounds the hunter came,
To cheer them on the vanished game ;
But, stumbling in the rugged dell,
The gallant horse exhausted fell.
The impatient rider strove in vain
To rouse him with the spur and rein,
For the good steed, his labours o'er,
Stretched his stiff limbs, to rise no more ;
Then, touched with pity and remorse,
He sorrowed o'er the expiring horse.
" I little thought, when first thy rein
I slacked upon the banks of Seine,
That Highland eagle e'er should feed
On thy fleet limbs, my matchless steed !
Woe worth the chase, woe worth the day,
That cost thy life, my gallant grey !"

Then through the dell his horn resounds,
From vain pursuit to call the hounds.
Back limped, with slow and cripple pace,
The sulky leaders of the chase ;

Lady of the Lake.

Close to their master's side they pressed,
With drooping tail and humbled crest ;
But still the dingle's hollow throat
Prolonged the swelling bugle-note.
The owlets started from their dream,
The eagles answered with their scream,
Round and around the sounds were cast,
Till echo seemed an answering blast ;
And on the hunter hied his way,
To join some comrades of the day ;
Yet often paused, so strange the road,
So wondrous were the scenes it showed.

The western waves of ebbing day
Rolled o'er the glen their level way ;
Each purple peak, each flinty spire,
Was bathed in floods of living fire.
But not a setting beam could glow
Within the dark ravines below,
Where twined the path, in shadow hid,
Round many a rocky pyramid,
Shooting abruptly from the dell
Its thunder-splintered pinnacle ;
Round many an insulated mass,
The native bulwarks of the pass,
Huge as the tower which builders vain
Presumptuous piled on Shinar's plain.

Lady of the Lake.

Their rocky summits, split and rent,
Formed turret, dome, or battlement,
Or seemed fantastically set
With cupola or minaret,
Wild crests as pagod ever decked,
Or mosque of Eastern architect.
Nor were these earth-born castles bare,
Nor lacked they many a banner fair;
For, from their shivered brows displayed,
Far o'er the unfathomable glade,
All twinkling with the dewdrop sheen,
The brier-rose fell in streamers green,
And creeping shrubs of thousand dyes,
Waved in the west wind's summer sighs.

Boon nature scattered, free and wild,
Each plant or flower, the mountain's child.
Here eglantine embalmed the air,
Hawthorn and hazel mingled there;
The primrose pale, and violet flower,
Found in each cliff a narrow bower;
Foxglove and nightshade, side by side,
Emblems of punishment and pride,
Grouped their dark hues with every stain
The weather-beaten crags retain.
With boughs that quaked at every breath,
Grey birch and aspen wept beneath;

Lady of the Lake.

Aloft, the ash and warrior oak
Cast anchor in the rifted rock;
And higher yet, the pine-tree hung
His shattered trunk, and frequent flung.
Where seemed the cliffs to meet on high,
His boughs athwart the narrowed sky.
Highest of all, where white peaks glanced,
Where glistening streamers waved and danced,
The wanderer's eye could barely view
The summer heaven's delicious blue;
So wondrous wild, the whole might seem
The scenery of a fairy dream.

Onward, amid the copse 'gan peep
A narrow inlet, still and deep,
Affording scarce such breadth of brim,
As served the wild-duck's brood to swim;
Lost for a space, through thickets veering,
But broader when again appearing,
Tall rocks and tufted knolls their face
Could on the dark-blue mirror trace;
And farther as the hunter strayed,
Still broader sweep its channels made.
The shaggy mounds no longer stood,
Emerging from entangled wood,
But wave-encircled, seemed to float,
Like castle girdled with its moat;

Lady of the Lake.

Yet broader floods extending still,
Divide them from their parent hill,
Till each, retiring, claims to be
An islet in an inland sea.

And now, to issue from the glen,
No pathway meets the wanderer's ken,

"Loch Katrine lay beneath him rolled."

Unless he climb, with footing nice,
A far projecting precipice.
The broom's tough roots his ladder made,
The hazel saplings lent their aid;

Lady of the Lake.

And thus an airy point he won,
Where, gleaming with the setting sun,
One burnished sheet of living gold,
Loch Katrine lay beneath him rolled ;
In all her length far winding lay,
With promontory, creek, and bay,
And islands that, empurpled bright,
Floated amid the livelier light ;
And mountains, that like giants stand,
To sentinel enchanted land.
High on the south, huge Ben Venue
Down to the lake in masses threw
Crags, knolls, and mounds, confusedly hurled,
The fragments of an earlier world ;
A wildering forest feathered o'er
His ruined sides and summit hoar,
While on the north, through middle air,
Ben An heaved high his forehead bare.

From the steep promontory gazed
The stranger, raptured and amazed,
And " What a scene were here," he cried,
" For princely pomp or churchman's pride !
On this bold brow, a lordly tower ;
In that soft vale, a lady's bower ;
On yonder meadow, far away,
The turrets of a cloister grey ;

Lady of the Lake.

How blithely might the bugle-horn
Chide, on the lake, the lingering morn!
How sweet, at eve, the lover's lute,
Chime, when the groves are still and mute!
And, when the midnight moon should lave
Her forehead in the silver wave,
How solemn on the ear would come
The holy matins' distant hum,
While the deep peal's commanding tone
Should wake, in yonder islet lone,
A sainted hermit from his cell,
To drop a bead with every knell—
And bugle, lute, and bell, and all,
Should each bewildered stranger call
To friendly feast and lighted hall.

" Blithe were it then to wander here!
But now,—beshrew yon nimble deer,—
Like that same hermit's thin and spare,
The copse must give my evening fare;
Some mossy bank my couch must be,
Some rustling oak my canopy.
Yet pass we that ;—the war and chase
Give little choice of resting-place ;
A summer night, in green-wood spent,
Were but to-morrow's merriment ;—

Lady of the Lake.

But hosts may in these wilds abound,
Such as are better missed than found :
To meet with Highland plunderers here
Were worse than loss of steed or deer.—
I am alone ;—my bugle strain
May call some straggler of the train ;
Or, fall the worse that may betide,
Ere now this falchion has been tried."

But scarce again his horn he wound,
When lo! forth starting at the sound,
From underneath an aged oak,
That slanted from the islet rock.
A Damsel guider of its way,
A little skiff shot to the bay,
That round the promontory steep
Led its deep line in graceful sweep,
Eddying, in almost viewless wave,
The weeping-willow twig to lave,
And kiss, with whispering sound and slow,
The beach of pebbles bright as snow.
The boat had touched the silver strand,
Just as the Hunter left his stand,
And stood concealed amid the brake,
To view this Lady of the Lake.
The maiden paused, as if again
She thought to catch the distant strain

Lady of the Lake.

With head up-raised, and look intent,
And eye and ear attentive bent,
And locks flung back, and lips apart,
Like monument of Grecian art.
In listening mood she seemed to stand,
The guardian Naiad of the strand.

*" And kiss, with whispering sound and slow,
The beach of pebbles bright as snow."*

And ne'er did Grecian chisel trace
A Nymph, a Naiad, or a Grace,
Of finer form, or lovelier face!
What though the sun, with ardent frown,
Had slightly tinged her cheek with brown,—

Lady of the Lake.

The sportive toil, which, short and light,
Had dyed her glowing hue so bright,
Served too in hastier swell to show
Short glimpses of a breast of snow;
What though no rule of courtly grace
To measured mood had trained her pace,—
A foot more light, a step more true,
Ne'er from the heath-flower dashed the dew;
E'en the slight hare-bell raised its head,
Elastic from her airy tread:
What though upon her speech there hung
The accents of the mountain tongue,—
Those silver sounds, so soft, so dear,
The listener held his breath to hear.

A chieftain's daughter seemed the maid;
Her satin snood, her silken plaid,
Her golden brooch, such birth betrayed.
And seldom was a snood amid
Such wild luxuriant ringlets hid,
Whose glossy black to shame might bring
The plumage of the raven's wing;
And seldom o'er a breast so fair,
Mantled a plaid with modest care,
And never brooch the folds combined
Above a heart more good and kind.

Lady of the Lake.

Her kindness and her worth to spy,
You need but gaze on Ellen's eye;
Not Katrine, in her mirror blue,
Gives back the shaggy banks more true,
Than every free-born glance confessed,
The guileless movements of her breast;
Whether joy danced in her dark eye,
Or woe or pity claimed a sigh,
Or filial love was growing there,
Or meek devotion poured a prayer,
Or tale of injury called forth
The indignant spirit of the north.
One only passion, unrevealed,
With maiden pride the maid concealed,
Yet not less purely felt the flame;—
O! need I tell that passion's name?

Morning on Loch Katrine.

—◦—

THE summer dawn's reflected hue
To purple changed Loch Katrine blue;
Mildly and soft the western breeze
Just kissed the lake, just stirred the trees,
And the pleased lake, like maiden coy,
Trembled, but dimpled not for joy;
The mountain-shadows on her breast
Were neither broken nor at rest;
In bright uncertainty they lie,
Like future joys to Fancy's eye.
The water-lily to the light
Her chalice reared of silver bright;
The doe awoke, and to the lawn,
Begemmed with dew-drops, led her fawn;
The grey mist left the mountain-side,
The torrent showed its glistening pride;
Invisible in fleckèd sky,
The lark sent down her revelry;
The blackbird and the speckled thrush
Good-morrow gave from brake and bush;
In answer cooed the cushat dove,
Her notes of peace, and rest, and love.

The Fiery Cross.

—⁘—

Fast as the fatal symbol flies,
In arms the huts and hamlets rise;
From winding glen, from upland brown,
They poured each hardy tenant down.
Nor slacked the messenger his pace;
He showed the sign, he named the place;
And, pressing forward like the wind,
Left clamour and surprise behind.
The fisherman forsook the strand,
The swarthy smith took dirk and brand,
With changèd cheer, the mower blithe
Left in the half-cut swathe his scythe;
The herds without a keeper strayed,
The plough was in mid-furrow stayed,
The falconer tossed his hawk away,
The hunter left the stag at bay;
Prompt at the signal of alarms,
Each son of Alpine rushed to arms;
So swept the tumult and affray
Along the margin of Achray.
Alas, thou lovely lake! that e'er
Thy banks should echo sounds of fear!

The Fiery Cross.

The rocks, the bosky thickets, sleep
So stilly on thy bosom deep,
The lark's blithe carol from the cloud,
Seems for the scene too gaily loud.

Speed, Malise, speed! the lake is passed,
Duncraggan's huts appear at last,
And peep, like moss-grown rocks, half seen,
Half hidden in the copse so green;
There mayst thou rest, thy labour done,
Their lord shall speed the signal on.—
As stoops the hawk upon his prey,
The henchman shot him down the way.
What woeful accents load the gale!
The funeral yell, the female wail!
A gallant hunter's sport is o'er,
A valiant warrior fights no more.
Who, in the battle or the chase,
At Roderick's side shall fill his place?—
Within the hall, where torches' ray
Supplies the excluded beams of day,
Lies Duncan on his lowly bier,
And o'er him streams his widow's tear.
His stripling son stands mournful by,
His youngest weeps, but knows not why;
The village maids and matrons round
The dismal coronach resound.

The Fiery Cross.

CORONACH.

He is gone on the mountain,
  He is lost to the forest,
Like a summer-dried fountain,
  When our need was the sorest.
The font, reappearing,
  From the rain-drops shall borrow,
But to us comes no cheering,
  To Duncan no morrow!

The hand of the reaper
  Takes the ears that are hoary,
But the voice of the weeper
  Wails manhood in glory;
The autumn winds rushing
  Waft the leaves that are searest,
But our flower was in flushing,
  When blighting was nearest.

Fleet foot on the correi,
  Sage counsel in cumber,
Red hand in the foray,
  How sound is thy slumber!
Like the dew on the mountain,
  Like the foam on the river,
Like the bubble on the fountain,
  Thou art gone, and for ever!

     ✢   ✢   ✢   ✢

The Fiery Cross.

Ben Ledi saw the Cross of Fire,
It glanced like lightning up Strath Ire.
O'er dale and hill the summons flew,
Not rest nor pause young Angus knew;
The tear that gathered in his eye,
He left the mountain-breeze to dry;
Until, where Teith's young waters roll,
Betwixt him and a wooded knoll,
That graced the sable strath with green,
The chapel of Saint Bride was seen.
Swollen was the stream, remote the bridge,
But Angus paused not on the edge;
Though the dark waves danced dizzily,
Though reeled his sympathetic eye,
He dashed amid the torrent's roar:
His right hand high the crosslet bore,
His left the pole-axe grasped, to guide
And stay his footing in the tide.
He stumbled twice—the foam splashed high,
With hoarser swell the stream raced by;
And had he fallen,—for ever there,
Farewell Duncraggan's orphan heir!
But still, as if in parting life,
Firmer he grasped the Cross of strife,
Until the opposing bank he gained,
And up the chapel pathway strained.

.

The Fiery Cross.

That summer morn had Roderick Dhu
Surveyed the skirts of Ben Venue,
And sent his scouts o'er hill and heath,
To view the frontiers of Menteith.
All backward came with news of truce;
Still lay each martial Græme and Bruce,
In Rednock courts no horsemen wait,
No banner waved on Cardross gate,
On Duchray's towers no beacon shone,
Nor scared the herons from Loch Con;
All seemed at peace.—Now, wot ye why
The Chieftain, with such anxious eye,
Ere to the muster he repair,
This western frontier scanned with care?—
In Ben Venue's most darksome cleft,
A fair, though cruel pledge was left;
For Douglas, to his promise true,
That morning from the isle withdrew,
And in a deep sequestered dell
Had sought a low and lonely cell.
By many a bard, in Celtic tongue,
Has Coir-nan-Uriskin been sung;
A softer name the Saxon gave,
And called the grot the Goblin-cave.

It was a wild and strange retreat,
As e'er was trod by outlaw's feet.

H

The Fiery Cross.

The dell, upon the mountain's crest,
Yawned like a gash on warrior's breast;
Its trench had stayed full many a rock,
Hurled by primeval earthquake shock
From Ben Venue's grey summit wild,
And here, in random ruin piled,
They frowned incumbent o'er the spot,
And formed the rugged sylvan grot.
The oak and birch, with mingled shade,
At noontide there a twilight made,
Unless when short and sudden shone
Some straggling beam on cliff or stone,
With such a glimpse as prophet's eye
Gains on thy depth, Futurity.
No murmur waked the solemn still,
Save tinkling of a fountain rill;
But when the wind chafed with the lake,
A sullen sound would upward break,
With dashing hollow voice, that spoke
The incessant war of wave and rock.
Suspended cliffs, with hideous sway,
Seemed nodding o'er the cavern grey.
From such a den the wolf had sprung,
In such the wild cat leaves her young;
Yet Douglas and his daughter fair
Sought, for a space, their safety there.
Grey Superstition's whisper dread
Debarred the spot to vulgar tread;

The Fiery Cross.

For there, she said, did fays resort,
And satyrs hold their sylvan court,
By moonlight tread their mystic maze,
And blast the rash beholder's gaze.

" *Above the Goblin-cave they go,*
Through the wild pass of Beal-nam-bo."

Now eve, with western shadows long,
Floated on Katrine bright and strong,
When Roderick, with a chosen few,
Repassed the heights of Ben Venue.
Above the Goblin-cave they go,
Through the wild pass of Beal-nam-bo;

The Fiery Cross.

The prompt retainers speed before,
To launch the shallop from the shore,
For 'cross Loch Katrine lies his way
To view the passes of Achray,
And place his clansmen in array.
Yet lags the Chief in musing mind,
Unwonted sight, his men behind.
A single page, to bear his sword,
Alone attended on his lord;
The rest their way through thickets break,
And soon await him by the lake.

The Prophecy.

—o—

" THE rose is fairest when 'tis budding new,
   And hope is brightest when it dawns from fears ;
The rose is sweetest washed with morning dew,
   And love is loveliest when embalmed in tears.
O wilding rose, whom fancy thus endears,
   I· bid your blossoms in my bonnet wave,
Emblem of hope and love through future years !"
   Thus spoke young Norman, heir of Armandave,
What time the sun arose on Vennachar's broad wave.

   Such fond conceit, half said, half sung,
   Love prompted to the bridegroom's tongue :
   All while he stripped the wild-rose spray,
   His axe and bow beside him lay,
   For on a pass 'twixt lake and wood,
   A wakeful sentinel he stood.
   Hark !—on the rock a footstep rung,
   And instant to his arms he sprung.
   " Stand, or thou diest !—What, Malise ?—soon
   Art thou returned from Braes of Doune.
   By thy keen step and glance I know,
   Thou bring'st us tidings of the foe."

The Prophecy.

(For while the Fiery Cross hied on,
On distant scout had Malise gone.)
"Where sleeps the Chief?" the henchman said.
"Apart, in yonder misty glade;
To his lone couch I'll be your guide."
Then called a slumberer by his side,
And stirred him with his slackened bow—
"Up, up, Glentarkin! rouse thee, ho!
We seek the Chieftain; on the track
Keep eagle watch till I come back."

Together up the pass they sped.
"What of the foeman?" Norman said.
"Varying reports from near and far,
This certain—that a band of war
Has for two day been ready boune,
At prompt command, to march from Doune;
King James, the while, with princely powers,
Holds revelry in Stirling towers.
Soon will this dark and gathering cloud
Speak on our glens in thunder loud.
Inured to bide such bitter bout,
The warrior's plaid may bear it out;
But, Norman, how wilt thou provide
A shelter for thy bonny bride?"
"What! know ye not that Roderick's care
To the lone isle hath caused repair

The Prophecy.

Each maid and matron of the clan,
And every child and aged man
Unfit for arms; and given his charge,
Nor skiff nor shallop, boat nor barge,
Upon these lakes shall float at large,
But all beside the islet moor,
That such dear pledge may rest secure?"—
"'Tis well advised—the Chieftain's plan
Bespeaks the father of his clan.
But wherefore sleeps Sir Roderick Dhu
Apart from all his followers true?"
"It is, because last evening-tide
Brian an augury hath tried,
Of that dread kind which must not be
Unless in dread extremity,
The Taghairm called; by which, afar,
Our sires foresaw the events of war.
Duncraggan's milk-white bull they slew,"——

MALISE.

"Ah! well the gallant brute I knew,
The choicest of the prey we had,
When swept our merry-men Gallangad.
His hide was snow, his horns were dark,
His red eye glowed like fiery spark;
So fierce, so tameless, and so fleet,
Sore did he cumber our retreat,

The Prophecy.

And kept our stoutest kernes in awe,
Even at the pass of Beal'maha.
But steep and flinty was the road,
And sharp the hurrying pikeman's goad ;
And when we came to Dennan's Row,
A child might scatheless stroke his brow."—

NORMAN.

" That bull was slain : his reeking hide
They stretched the cataract beside,
Whose waters their wild tumult toss
Adown the black and craggy boss
Of that huge cliff, whose ample verge
Tradition calls the Hero's Targe.
Couched on a shelve beneath its brink,
Close where the thundering torrents sink,
Rocking beneath their headlong sway,
And drizzled by the ceaseless spray,
'Midst groan of rock, and roar of stream,
The wizard waits prophetic dream.
Nor distant rests the Chief:—but hush !
See, gliding slow through mist and bush,
The Hermit gains yon rock, and stands
To gaze upon our slumbering bands.
Seems he not, Malise, like a ghost,
That hovers o'er a slaughtered host ?

" *Whose waters their wild tumult toss*
Adown the Hack and craggy boss
Of that huge cliff, whose ample verge
Tradition calls the Hero's Targe."

The Prophecy.

Or raven on the blasted oak,
That, watching while the deer is broke,
His morsel claims with sullen croak?"

MALISE.

"Peace! peace! to other than to me,
Thy words were evil augury;
But still I hold Sir Roderick's blade
Clan-Alpine's omen and her aid,
Not aught that, gleaned from heaven or hell,
Yon fiend-begotten monk can tell.
The Chieftain joins him, see—and now,
Together they descend the brow."—

And, as they came, with Alpine's Lord
The Hermit Monk held solemn word:
"Roderick! it is a fearful strife,
For man endowed with mortal life,
Whose shroud of sentient clay can still
Feel feverish pang and fainting chill,
Whose eye can stare in stony trance,
Whose hair can rouse like warrior's lance,—
'Tis hard for such to view, unfurled,
The curtain of the future world.
Yet, witness every quaking limb,
My sunken pulse, mine eyeballs dim,

The Prophecy.

My soul with harrowing anguish torn,
This for my chieftain have I borne!
The shapes that sought my fearful couch,
A human tongue may ne'er avouch;
No mortal man,—save he, who, bred
Between the living and the dead,
Is gifted beyond nature's law,
Had e'er survived to say he saw.
At length the fateful answer came,
In characters of living flame!
Not spoke in word, nor blazed in scroll,
But borne and branded on my soul;—
WHICH SPILLS THE FOREMOST FOEMAN'S LIFE,
THAT PARTY CONQUERS IN THE STRIFE."

The Combat.

—*o*—

THE chief in silence strode before,
And reached that torrent's sounding shore,
Which, daughter of three mighty lakes,
From Vennachar in silver breaks,
Sweeps through the plain, and ceaseless mines
On Bochastle the mouldering lines,
Where Rome, the Empress of the world,
Of yore her eagle wings unfurled.
And here his course the Chieftain stayed,
Threw down his target and his plaid,
And to the Lowland warrior said :—
" Bold Saxon ! to his promise just,
Vich-Alpine has discharged his trust.
This murderous chief, this ruthless man,
This head of a rebellious clan,
Hath led thee safe, through watch and ward,
Far past Clan-Alpine's outmost guard.
Now, man to man, and steel to steel,
A chieftain's vengeance thou shalt feel.
See, here, all vantageless I stand,
Armed, like thyself, with single brand ;

The Combat.

For this is Coilantogle ford,
And thou must keep thee with thy sword."—

The Saxon paused :—" I ne'er delayed,
When foeman bade me draw my blade ;
Nay more, brave Chief, I vowed thy death :
Yet sure thy fair and generous faith,
And my deep debt for life preserved,
A better meed have well deserved :—
Can nought but blood our feud atone ?
Are there no means ?"—" No, Stranger, none !
And hear,—to fire thy flagging zeal,—
The Saxon cause rests on thy steel ;
For thus spoke Fate by prophet bred
Between the living and the dead ;
' Who spills the foremost foeman's life,
His party conquers in the strife.' "—
" Then, by my word," the Saxon said,
" The riddle is already read.
Seek yonder brake beneath the cliff—
There lies Red Murdoch, stark and stiff.
Thus Fate has solved her prophecy ;
Then yield to Fate, and not to me.
To James, at Stirling, let us go,
When, if thou wilt, be still his foe,
Or if the King shall not agree
To grant thee grace and favour free,

The Combat.

I plight mine honour, oath, and word,
That, to thy native strengths restored,
With each advantage shalt thou stand,
That aids thee now to guard thy land."—

'Dark lightning flashed from Roderick's eye—
"Soars thy presumption, then, so high,
Because a wretched kerne ye slew,
Homage to name to Roderick Dhu?
He yields not, he, to man nor Fate!
Thou add'st but fuel to my hate:—
My clansman's blood demands revenge.—
Not yet prepared?—By Heaven, I change
My thought, and hold thy valour light
As that of some vain carpet-knight,
Who ill deserved my courteous care,
And whose best boast is but to wear
A braid of his fair lady's hair."
" I thank thee, Roderick, for the word!
It nerves my heart, it steels my sword;
For I have sworn this braid to stain
In the best blood that warms thy vein.
Now, truce, farewell! and ruth begone!—
Yet think not that by thee alone,
Proud Chief! can courtesy be shown;
Though not from copse, or heath, or cairn,
Start at my whistle clansmen stern,

The Combat.

Of this small horn one feeble blast
Would fearful odds against thee cast.
But fear not—doubt not—which thou wilt—
We try this quarrel hilt to hilt."—
Then each at once his falchion drew,
Each on the ground his scabbard threw,
Each looked to sun, and stream, and plain,
As what they ne'er might see again;
Then foot, and point, and eye opposed,
In dubious strife they darkly closed.

Ill fared it then with Roderick Dhu,
That on the field his targe he threw,
Whose brazen studs and tough bull-hide
Had death so often dashed aside;
For, trained abroad his arms to wield,
Fitz-James's blade was sword and shield;
He practised every pass and ward,
To thrust, to strike, to feint, to guard;
While, less expert, though stronger far,
The Gael maintained unequal war.
Three times in closing strife they stood,
And thrice the Saxon sword drank blood;
No stinted draught, no scanty tide,
The gushing flood the tartans dyed.
Fierce Roderick felt the fatal drain,
And showered his blows like wintry rain;

The Combat.

And, as firm rock, or castle-roof,
Against the winter shower is proof,
The foe, invulnerable still,
Foiled his wild rage by steady skill;
Till, at advantage ta'en, his brand
Forced Roderick's weapon from his hand,
And, backwards borne upon the lea,
Brought the proud Chieftain to his knee..

"Now, yield thee, or, by Him who made
The world, thy heart's blood dyes my blade!"
"Thy threats, thy mercy, I defy!
Let recreant yield who fears to die."—
Like adder darting from his coil,
Like wolf that dashes through the toil,
Like mountain-cat who guards her young,
Full at Fitz-James's throat he sprung,
Received, but recked not of a wound,
And locked his arms his foeman round.—
Now, gallant Saxon, hold thine own!
No maiden's hand is round thee thrown!
That desperate grasp thy frame might feel
Through bars of brass and triple steel!—
They tug, they strain!—down, down, they go,
The Gael above, Fitz-James below.
The Chieftain's gripe his throat compressed,
His knee was planted on his breast;

The Combat.

His clotted locks he backward threw,
Across his brow his hand he drew,
From blood and mist to clear his sight,
Then gleamed aloft his dagger bright!—
But hate and fury ill supplied
The stream of life's exhausted tide,
And all too late the advantage came,
To turn the odds of deadly game;
For, while the dagger gleamed on high,
Reeled soul and sense, reeled brain and eye.
Down came the blow! but in the heath
The erring blade found bloodless sheath.
The struggling foe may now unclasp
The fainting Chief's relaxing grasp;
Unwounded from the dreadful close,
But breathless all, Fitz-James arose.

A Farewell.

———o———

Harp of the North, farewell! The hills grow dark,
  On purple peaks a deeper shade descending;
In twilight copse the glow-worm lights her spark,
  The deer, half-seen, are to the covert wending.
Resume thy wizard elm! the fountain lending,
  And the wild breeze, thy wilder minstrelsy;
Thy numbers sweet with Nature's vespers blending,
  With distant echo from the fold and lea,
And herd-boy's evening pipe and hum of housing bee.

Yet, once again, farewell, thou Minstrel Harp!
  Yet, once again, forgive my feeble sway,
And little reck I of the censure sharp
  May idly cavil at an idle lay.
Much have I owed thy strains on life's long way,
  Through secret woes the world has never known,
When on the weary night dawned wearier day,
  And bitterer was the grief devoured alone.
That I o'eflive such woes, Enchantress! is thine own.

A Farewell.

Hark! as my lingering footsteps slow retire,
  Some Spirit of the Air has waked thy string!
'Tis now a Seraph bold, with touch of fire,
  'Tis now the brush of Fairy's frolic wing.
Receding now, the dying numbers ring
  Fainter and fainter down the rugged dell,
And now the mountain breezes scarcely bring
  A wandering witch-note of the distant spell—
And now 'tis silent all!—Enchantress, fare thee well!

SCENES FROM "LORD OF THE ISLES."

—— o ——

Introduction to Canto Fourth.

STRANGER! if e'er thine ardent step hath traced
    The northern realms of ancient Caledon,
Where the proud Queen of Wilderness hath placed,
    By lake and cataract, her lonely throne;
Sublime but sad delight thy soul hath known,
    Gazing on pathless glen and mountain high,
Listing where from the cliffs the torrents thrown
    Mingle their echoes with the eagle's cry,
And with the sounding lake, and with the moaning sky.

Introduction to Canto Fourth.

Yes! 'twas sublime, but sad.—The loneliness
    Loaded thy heart, the desert tired thine eye;
And strange and awful fears began to press
    Thy bosom with a stern solemnity.
Then hast thou wished some woodman's cottage nigh,
    Something that showed of life, though low and mean;
Glad sight, its curling wreath of smoke to spy,
    Glad sound, its cock's blithe carol would have been,
Or children whooping wild beneath the willows green.

Such are the scenes, where savage grandeur wakes
    An awful thrill that softens into sighs;
Such feelings rouse them by dim Rannoch's lakes,
    In dark Glencoe such gloomy raptures rise:
Or further, where, beneath the northern skies,
    Chides wild Loch Eribol his caverns hoar—
But, be the minstrel judge, they yield the prize
    Of desert dignity to that dread shore,
That sees grim Coolin rise, and hears Coriskin roar.

" In dark Glencoe such gloomy raptures rise."

Skye.

——o——

With Bruce and Ronald bides the tale.
To favouring winds they gave the sail,
Till Mull's dark headlands scarce they knew,
And Ardnamurchan's hills were blue.
But then the squalls blew close and hard,
And, fain to strike the galley's yard,
    And take them to the oar,
With these rude seas, in weary plight,
They strove the livelong day and night,
Nor till the dawning had a sight
    Of Skye's romantic shore.
Where Coolin stoops him to the west,
They saw upon his shivered crest
    The sun's arising gleam;
But such the labour and delay,
Ere they were moored in Scarigh bay,
(For calmer heaven compelled to stay,)
    He shot a western beam.
Then Ronald said,—"If true mine eye,
These are the savage wilds that lie
North of Strathnardill and Dunskye;
    No human foot comes here,

Skye.

And, since these adverse breezes blow,
If my good Liege love hunter's bow,
What hinders that on land we go,
  And strike a mountain deer?
Allan, my Page, shall with us wend;
A bow full deftly can he bend,
And, if we meet a herd, may send
  A shaft shall mend our cheer."—
Then each took bow and bolts in hand,
Their row-boat launched and leapt to land,
  And left their skiff and train,
Where a wild stream, with headlong shock,
Came brawling down its bed of rock,
  To mingle with the main.

A while their route they silent made,
  As men who stalk for mountain deer,
Till the good Bruce to Ronald said,
  "St. Mary! what a scene is here!
I've traversed many a mountain-strand,
Abroad and in my native land,
And it has been my lot to tread
Where safety more than pleasure led;
  Thus, many a waste I've wandered o'er,
  Clombe many a crag, crossed many a moor;
  But, by my halidome,

Skye.

A scene so rude, so wild as this,
Yet so sublime in barrenness,
Ne'er did my wandering footsteps press,
　　Where'er I happed to roam."—

No marvel thus the Monarch spake;
　　For rarely human eye has known
A scene so stern as that dread lake,
　　With its dark ledge of barren stone.
Seems that primeval earthquake's sway
Hath rent a strange and shattered way
　　Through the rude bosom of the hill,
And that each naked precipice,
Sable ravine and dark abyss,
　　Tells of the outrage still.
The wildest glen, but this, can show
Some touch of Nature's genial glow:
On high Benmore green mosses grow,
And heathbells bud in deep Glencoe,
　　And copse on Cruchan-Ben;
But here, above, around, below,
　　On mountain or in glen,
Nor tree, nor shrub, nor plant, nor flower,
Nor aught of vegetative power,
　　The weary eye may ken.
For all is rocks at random thrown,
Black waves, bare crags, and banks of stone,
　　As if were here denied

Skye.

The summer sun, the spring's sweet dew,
That clothe with many a varied hue
    The bleakest mountain-side.

And wilder, forward as they wound,
Were the proud cliffs and lake profound.
Huge terraces of granite black
Afforded rude and cumbered track ;
    For from the mountain hoar,
Hurled headlong in some night of fear,
When yelled the wolf and fled the deer,
    Loose crags had toppled o'er ;
And some, chance-poised and balanced, lay,
So that a stripling arm might sway
    A mass no host could raise,
In Nature's rage at random thrown.
Yet trembling like the Druid's stone
    On its precarious base.
The evening mists, with ceaseless change,
Now clothed the mountains' lofty range,
    Now left their foreheads bare,
And round the skirts their mantle furled,
Or on the sable waters curled,
Or, on the eddying breezes whirled,
    Dispersed in middle air.
And oft, condensed, at once they lower,
When, brief and fierce, the mountain shower
    Pours like a torrent down,

Skye.

And when return the sun's glad beams,
Whitened with foam a thousand streams
    Leap from the mountain's crown.

" *That to the evening sun uplifts*
   The griesly gulfs and slaty rifts.

Coriskin call the dark lake's name,
Coolin the ridge, as bards proclaim."

" This lake," said Bruce, " whose barriers drear
Are precipices sharp and sheer,
Yielding no track for goat or deer,
    Save the black shelves we tread,

Skye.

How term you its dark waves? and how
Yon northern mountain's pathless brow,
    And yonder peak of dread,
That to the evening sun uplifts
The griesly gulfs and slaty rifts,
    Which seam its shivered head?"—
"Coriskin call the dark lake's name,
Coolin the ridge, as bards proclaim,
From old Cuchullin, chief of fame.
But bards, familiar in our isles
Rather with Nature's frowns than smiles,
Full oft their careless humours please
By sportive names for scenes like these.
I would old Torquil were to show
His Maidens with their breasts of snow,
Or that my noble Liege were nigh
To hear his Nurse sing lullaby!
(The Maids—tall cliffs with breakers white,
The Nurse—a torrent's roaring might);
Or that your eye could see the mood
Of Corrievreken's whirlpool rude,
When dons the Hag her whitened hood—
'Tis thus our islesmen's fancy frames,
For scenes so stern, fantastic names."—

Answered the Bruce, "And musing mind
Might here a graver moral find.

Skye.

These mighty cliffs, that heave on high
Their naked brows to middle sky,
Indifferent to the sun or snow,
Where nought can fade, and nought can blow,
May they not mark a Monarch's fate,—
Raised high 'mid storms of strife and state,
Beyond life's lowlier pleasures placed,
His soul a rock, his heart a waste?

The Voyage.

—*o*—

Coriskin dark and Coolin high
Echoed the dirge's doleful cry;
Along that sable lake passed slow,—
Fit scene for such a sight of woe,—
The sorrowing islesmen, as they bore
The murdered Allan to the shore.
At every pause, with dismal shout,
Their coronach of grief rung out.
And ever, when they moved again,
The pipes resumed their clamorous strain,
And, with the pibroch's shrilling wail,
Mourned the young heir of Donagaile.
Round and around, from cliff and cave,
His answer stern old Coolin gave,
Till high upon his misty side
Languished the mournful notes, and died.
For never sounds, by mortal made,
Attained his high and haggard head,
That echoes but the tempest's moan,
Or the deep thunder's rending groan.

The Voyage.

Merrily, merrily, bounds the bark,
    She bounds before the gale,
The mountain breeze from Ben-na-darch
    Is joyous in her sail!
With fluttering sound like laughter hoarse
    The cords and canvas strain,
The waves, divided by her force,
In rippling eddies chased her course,
    As if they laughed again.
Not down the breeze more blithely flew,
Skimming the wave, the light sea-mew,
    Than that gay galley bore
Her course upon that favouring wind,
And Coolin's crest has sunk behind,
    And Slapin's caverned shore.
'Twas then that warlike signals wake
Dunscaith's dark towers and Eisord's lake,
And soon from Cavilgarrigh's head
Thick wreaths of eddying smoke were spread;
A summons these of war and wrath
To the brave clans of Sleate and Strath,
    And, ready at the sight,
Each warrior to his weapons sprung,
And targe upon his shoulder flung,
    Impatient for the fight.
Mac-Kinnon's Chief, in warfare gray,
Had charge to muster their array,
And guide their barks to Brodick-Bay.

The Voyage.

Signal of Ronald's high command,
A beacon gleamed o'er sea and land,
From Canna's tower, that, steep and gray,
Like falcon nest o'erhangs the bay.
Seek not the giddy crag to climb,
To view the turret scathed by time;
It is a task of doubt and fear
To aught but goat or mountain-deer.
　　But rest thee on the silver beach,
　　And let the aged herdsman teach
　　　　His tale of former day;
　　His cur's wild clamour he shall chide,
　　And for thy seat by ocean's side
　　　　His varied plaid display;
　　Then tell, with Canna's Chieftain came,
　　In ancient times, a foreign dame
　　　　To yonder turret gray.
Stern was her Lord's suspicious mind,
Who in so rude a jail confined
　　So soft and fair a thrall!
And oft, when moon on ocean slept,
That lovely lady sate and wept
　　Upon the Castle wall,
And turned her eye to southern climes,
And thought perchance of happier times,
And touched her lute by fits, and sung
Wild ditties in her native tongue.
And still, when on the cliff and bay,

The Voyage.

Placid and pale the moonbeams play,
    And every breeze is mute,
Upon the lone Hebridean's ear
Steals a strange pleasure mixed with fear,
While from that cliff he seems to hear
    The murmur of a lute,
And sounds, as of a captive lone,
That mourns her woes in tongue unknown.—
Strange is the tale—but all too long
Already hath it stayed the song—
    Yet who may pass them by,
That crag and tower in ruins gray, ·
Nor to their hapless tenant pay
    The tribute of a sigh!

Merrily, merrily bounds the bark
    O'er the broad ocean driven,
Her path by Ronin's mountains dark
    The steersman's hand has given.
And Ronin's mountains dark have sent
    Their hunters to the shore,
And each his ashen bow unbent,
    And gave his pastime o'er,
And at the Island Lord's command,
For hunting-spear took warrior's brand.
On Scoor-Eigg next a warning light
Summoned her warriors to the fight;

The Voyage.

A numerous race, ·ere stern Macleod
O'er their bleak shores in vengeance strode,
When all in vain the ocean cave
Its refuge to his victims gave.
The Chief, relentless in his wrath,
With blazing heath blockades the path :
In dense and stifling volumes rolled,
The vapour filled the caverned Hold!
The warrior-threat, the infant's plain,
The mother's screams, were heard in vain ;
The vengeful Chief maintains his fires,
Till in the vault a tribe expires!
The bones which strew that cavern's gloom,
Too well attest their dismal doom.

Merrily, merrily goes the bark
    On a breeze from the northward free.
So shoots through the morning sky the lark,
    Or the swan through the summer sea.
The shores of Mull on the eastward lay,
And Ulva dark and Colonsay,
And all the group of islets gay
    That guard famed Staffa round.
Then all unknown its columns rose,
Where dark and undisturbed repose
    The cormorant had found,

" Nature herself, it seemed, would raise
A Minster to her Maker's praise!
Not for a meaner use ascend
Her columns, or her arches bend:
Nor of a theme less solemn tells
That mighty surge that ebbs and swells."

And the shy seal had quiet home,
And weltered in that wondrous dome,
Where, as to shame the temples decked
By skill of earthly architect,
Nature herself, it seemed, would raise
A Minster to her Maker's praise!
Not for a meaner use ascend
Her columns, or her arches bend;

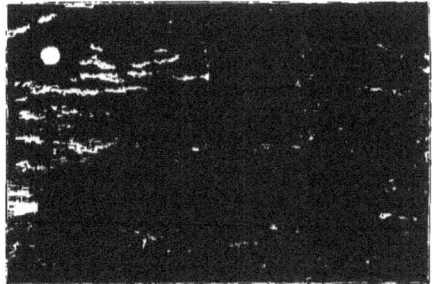

" Old Iona's holy fane."

Nor of a theme less solemn tells
That mighty surge that ebbs and swells,
And still, between each awful pause,
From the high vault an answer draws,
In varied tone prolonged and high,
That mocks the organ's melody.
Nor doth its entrance front in vain
To old Iona's holy fane,

The Voyage.

That Nature's voice might seem to say,
"Well hast thou done, frail Child of clay!
Thy humble powers that stately shrine
Tasked high and hard—but witness mine!"

Merrily, merrily goes the bark,
    Before the gale she bounds;
So darts the dolphin from the shark,
    Or the deer before the hounds.
They left Loch Tua on their lee,
And they wakened the men of the wild Tiree,
    And the Chief of the sandy Coll;
They paused not at Columba's isle,
Though pealed the bells from the holy pile
    With long and measured toll;
No time for matin or for mass,
And the sounds of the holy summons pass
    Away in the billows' roll.
Lochbuie's fierce and warlike Lord
Their signal saw, and grasped his sword,
And verdant Islay called her host,
And the clans of Jura's rugged coast
    Lord Ronald's call obey,
And Scarba's isle, whose tortured shore
Still rings to Corrievreken's roar,
    And lonely Colonsay;

The Voyage.

—Scenes sung by him who sings no more!
His bright and brief career is o'er,
    And mute his tuneful strains ;
Quenched is his lamp of varied lore,
That loved the light of song to pour ;
A distant and a deadly shore
    Has LEYDEN'S cold remains!

Ever the breeze blows merrily,
But the galley ploughs no more the sea.
Lest, rounding wild Cantire, they meet·
The Southern foemen's watchful fleet,
    They held unwonted way ;—
Up Tarbat's western lake they bore,
Then dragged their bark the isthmus o'er,
As far as Kilmaconnel's shore,
    Upon the eastern bay.
It was a wondrous sight to see
Topmast and pennon glitter free,
High raised above the greenwood tree,
As on dry land the galley moves,
By cliff and copse and alder groves.
Deep import from that selcouth sign,
Did many a mountain Seer divine,
  For ancient legends told the Gael,
  That when a royal bark should sail
    O'er Kilmaconnel moss,

The Voyage.

Old Albyn should in fight prevail,
And every foe should faint and quail
   Before her silver Cross,

" Gave his grim peaks a greeting kind,
And bade Loch Ranza smile."

Now launched once more, the inland sea
They furrow with fair augury,
   And steer for Arran's isle ;
The sun, ere yet he sunk behind
Ben Ghoil, " The Mountain of the Wind,"
Gave his grim peaks a greeting kind,
   And bade Loch Ranza smile.

In Arran.

Thither their destined course they drew;
It seemed the Isle her Monarch knew,
So brilliant was the landward view,
    The ocean so serene;
Each puny wave in diamonds rolled
O'er the calm deep, where hues of gold
    With azure strove and green.
The hill, the vale, the tree, the tower,
Glowed with the tints of evening's hour,
    The beach was silver sheen;
The wind breathed soft as lover's sigh,
And, oft renewed, seemed oft to die,
    With breathless pause between.
Oh, who, with speech of war and woes,
Would wish to break the soft repose
    Of such enchanting scene!

Autumn on the Tweed.

—♪—

Autumn departs—but still his mantle's fold
 Rests on the groves of noble Somerville,
Beneath a shroud of russet dropped with gold
 Tweed and his tributaries mingle still;
Hoarser the wind, and deeper sounds the rill.
 Yet lingering notes of sylvan music swell,
The deep-toned cushat, and the redbreast shrill;
 And yet some tints of summer splendour tell
When the broad sun sinks down on Ettricke's western fell.

Autumn departs—from Gala's fields no more
 Come rural sounds our kindred banks to cheer;
Blent with the stream, and gale that wafts it o'er.
 No more the distant reapers' mirth we hear.
The last blithe shout hath died upon our ear,
 And harvest-home hath hushed the clanging wain.
On the waste hill no forms of life appear,
 Save where, sad laggard of the autumnal train,
Some age-struck wanderer gleans few ears of scattered grain.

Autumn on the Tweed.

Deem'st thou these saddened scenes have pleasure still,
   Lovest thou through Autumn's fading realms to stray,
To see the heath-flower withered on the hill,
   To listen to the woods' expiring lay,
To note the red leaf shivering on the spray,
   To mark the last bright tints the mountain stain,
On the waste fields to trace the gleaner's way,
   And moralise on mortal joy and pain ?—
Oh, if such scenes thou lovest, scorn not the minstrel strain !

No! do not scorn, although its hoarser note
   Scarce with the cushat's homely song can vie,
Though faint its beauties as the tints remote
   That gleam through mist in Autumn's evening sky,
And few as leaves that tremble, sear and dry,
   When wild November hath his bugle wound ;
Nor mock my toil—a lonely gleaner I,
   Through fields time-wasted, on sad inquest bound,
Where happier bards of yore have richer harvest found.

The Sun upon the Weirdlaw Hill.

——o——

THE sun upon the Weirdlaw Hill,
   In Ettrick's vale, is sinking sweet;
The westland wind is hush and still,
   The lake lies sleeping at my feet.
Yet not the landscape to mine eye
   Bears those bright hues that once it bore;
Though evening, with her richest dye,
   Flames o'er the hills of Ettrick's shore.

With listless look along the plain,
   I see Tweed's silver current glide,
And coldly mark the holy fane
   Of Melrose rise in ruin'd pride.
The quiet lake, the balmy air,
   The hill, the stream, the tower, the tree,—
Are they still such as once they were?
   Or is the dreary change in me?

The Sun upon the Weirdlaw Hill.

Alas, the warp'd and broken board,
   How can it bear the painter's dye!
The harp of strain'd and tuneless chord,
   How to the minstrel's skill reply!
To aching eyes each landscape lowers,
   To feverish pulse each gale blows chill;
And Araby's or Eden's bowers
   Were barren as this moorland hill.

The Maid of Neidpath.

———0———

THERE is a tradition in Tweeddale, that when Neidpath Castle, near
Peebles, was inhabited by the Earls of March, a mutual passion subsisted
between a daughter of that noble family and a son of the laird of Tushielaw, in Ettricke Forest. As the alliance was thought unsuitable by her
parents, the young man went abroad. During his absence, the lady fell
into a consumption, and at length, as the only means of saving her life,
her father consented that her lover should be recalled. On the day
when he was expected to pass through Peebles on the road to Tushielaw,
the young lady, though much exhausted, caused herself to be carried to
the balcony of a house in Peebles belonging to the family, that she
might see him as he rode past. Her anxiety and eagerness gave such
force to her organs that she is said to have distinguished his horse's
footsteps at an incredible distance. But Tushielaw, unprepared for the
change in her appearance, and not expecting to see her in that place,
rode on without recognising her, or even slackening his pace. The lady
was unable to support the shock, and, after a short struggle, died in the
arms of her attendants. There is an incident similar to this traditional
tale in Count Hamilton's " Fleur d'Epine."

The Maid of Neidpath.

Oh! lovers' eyes are sharp to see,
 And lovers' ears in hearing;
And love, in life's extremity,
 Can lend an hour of cheering.
Disease had been in Mary's bower,
 And slow decay from mourning,
Though now she sits on Neidpath's tower
 To watch her love's returning.

All sunk and dim her eyes so bright,
 Her form decayed by pining,
Till through her wasted hand, at night,
 You saw the taper shining;
By fits, a sultry hectic hue
 Across her cheek was flying;
By fits, so ashy pale she grew,
 Her maidens thought her dying.

Yet keenest powers, to see and hear,
 Seemed in her frame residing;
Before the watch-dog pricked his ear,
 She heard her lover's riding;
Ere scarce a distant form was kenned,
 She knew, and waved to greet him;
And o'er the battlement did bend,
 As on the wing to meet him.

The Maid of Neidpath.

He came—he passed—a heedless gaze,
    As o'er some stranger glancing,
Her welcome spoke, in faltering phrase,
    Lost in his courser's prancing—
The castle arch, whose hollow tone
    Returns each whisper spoken,
Could scarcely catch the feeble moan,
    Which told her heart was broken.

ROBERT   BURNS

" While tumbling brown, the burn comes down,
And roars frae bank to brae."

Winter: A Dirge.

—— o ——

THE wintry west extends his blast,
  And hail and rain does blaw;
Or, the stormy north sends driving forth
  The blinding sleet and snaw:
While tumbling brown, the burn comes down,
  And roars frae bank to brae;
And bird and beast in covert rest,
  And pass the heartless day.

Winter.

"The sweeping blast, the sky o'ercast,"
　　The joyless winter-day,
Let others fear, to me more dear
　　Than all the pride of May:
The tempest's howl, it soothes my soul,
　　My griefs it seems to join;
The leafless trees my fancy please,
　　Their fate resembles mine!

Thou power Supreme, whose mighty scheme
　　These woes of mine fulfil,
Here, firm, I rest, they must be best,
　　Because they are Thy will!
Then all I want (oh, do Thou grant
　　This one request of mine!)
Since to enjoy Thou dost deny,
　　Assist me to resign.

The Cotter's Saturday Night.[1]

INSCRIBED TO ROBERT AIKEN, ESQ.

——o——

My loved, my honour'd, much-respected friend!
  No mercenary bard his homage pays;
With honest pride, I scorn each selfish end:
  My dearest meed, a friend's esteem and praise:
To you I sing, in simple Scottish lays,
  The lowly train in life's sequester'd scene;
The native feelings strong, the guileless ways:
  What Aiken in a cottage would have been;
Ah! though his worth unknown, far happier there, I ween!

November chill blaws loud wi' angry sugh;
  The short'ning winter-day is near a close;
The miry beasts retreating frae the pleugh;
  The black'ning trains o' craws to their repose;
The toil-worn cotter frae his labour goes,
  This night his weekly moil is at an end,
Collects his spades, his mattocks, and his hoes,
  Hoping the morn in ease and rest to spend,
And, weary, o'er the moor his course does hameward bend.

The Cotter's Saturday Night.

At length his lonely cot appears in view,
    Beneath the shelter of an aged tree ;
Th' expectant wee things, toddlin', stacher through
    To meet their dad, wi' flichterin' noise and glee.
His wee bit ingle, blinking bonnily,
    His clean hearthstane, his thrifty wifie's smile,
The lisping infant prattling on his knee,
    Does a' his weary carking cares beguile,
And makes him quite forget his labour and his toil.

Belyve, the elder bairns come drapping in,
    At service out, among the farmers roun' :
Some ca' the pleugh, some herd, some tentie rin
    A canny errand to a neibor town :
Their eldest hope, their Jenny, woman grown,
    In youthfu' bloom, love sparkling in her ee,
Comes hame, perhaps to show a braw new gown,
    Or deposit her sair-won penny-fee,
To help her parents dear, if they in hardship be.

Wi' joy unfeign'd, brothers and sisters meet,
    And each for other's weelfare kindly speers :
The social hours, swift-wing'd, unnoticed, fleet ;
    Each tells the uncos that he sees or hears ;
The parents, partial, eye their hopeful years ;
    Anticipation forward points the view.
The mother, wi' her needle and her shears,
    Gars auld claes look amaist as weel 's the new—
The father mixes a' wi' admonition due.

The Cotter's Saturday Night.

Their master's and their mistress's command,
    The younkers a' are warned to obey;
And mind their labours wi' an eydent hand,
    And ne'er, though out o' sight, to jauk or play:
"And oh! be sure to fear the Lord alway!
    And mind your duty, duly, morn and night!
Lest in temptation's path ye gang astray,
    Implore His counsel and assisting might:
They never sought in vain that sought the Lord aright!"

But, hark! a rap comes gently to the door;
    Jenny, wha kens the meaning o' the same,
Tells how a neibor lad cam o'er the moor,
    To do some errands, and convoy her hame.
The wily mother sees the conscious flame
    Sparkle in Jenny's ee, and flush her cheek,
Wi' heart-struck anxious care, inquires his name,
    While Jenny hafflins is afraid to speak;
Weel pleased the mother hears it's nae wild, worthless rake.

Wi' kindly welcome, Jenny brings him ben;
    A strappin' youth, he taks the mother's eye;
Blythe Jenny sees the visit's no ill ta'en;
    The father cracks of horses, pleughs, and kye.
The youngster's artless heart o'erflows wi' joy,
    But blate and lathefu', scarce can weel behave;
The mother, wi' a woman's wiles, can spy
    What makes the youth sae bashfu' and sae grave;
Weel pleased to think her bairn's respected like the lave.

The Cotter's Saturday Night.

O happy love!—where love like this is found!—
    O heart-felt raptures!—bliss beyond compare!
I've pacèd much this weary, mortal round,
    And sage experience bids me this declare—
" If Heaven a draught of heavenly pleasure spare,
    One cordial in this melancholy vale,
'Tis when a youthful, loving, modest pair,
    In other's arms, breathe out the tender tale,
Beneath the milk-white thorn that scents the evening gale.'

Is there, in human form, that bears a heart,
    A wretch! a villain! lost to love and truth!
That can, with studied, sly, ensnaring art,
    Betray sweet Jenny's unsuspecting youth?
Curse on his perjured arts! dissembling smooth!
    Are honour, virtue, conscience, all exiled?
Is there no pity, no relenting ruth,
    Points to the parents fondling o'er their child?
Then paints the ruin'd maid, and their distraction wild!

But now the supper crowns their simple board,
    The halesome parritch, chief of Scotia's food:
The soupe their only hawkie does afford,
    That 'yont the hallan snugly chows her cood:
The dame brings forth, in complimental mood,
    To grace the lad, her weel-hain'd kebbuck, fell,
And aft he's prest, and aft he ca's it guid:
    The frugal wifie, garrulous, will tell,
How 'twas a townmond auld, sin' lint was i' the bell.

The Cotter's Saturday Night.

The cheerfu' supper done, wi' serious face,
    They, round the ingle, form a circle wide;
The sire turns o'er, wi' patriarchal grace,
    The big ha' Bible, ance his father's pride;
His bonnet rev'rently is laid aside,
    His lyart haffets wearing thin and bare;
Those strains that once did sweet in Zion glide,
    He wales a portion with judicious care;
And "Let us worship God!" he says, with solemn air.

They chant their artless notes in simple guise;
    They tune their hearts, by far the noblest aim:
Perhaps "Dundee's" wild-warbling measures rise,
    Or plaintive "Martyrs," worthy of the name;
Or noble "Elgin" beets the heaven-ward flame,
    The sweetest far of Scotia's holy lays;
Compared with these, Italian trills are tame;
    The tickled ear no heartfelt raptures raise;
Nae unison hae they with our Creator's praise.

The priest-like father reads the sacred page,
    How Abram was the Friend of God on high,
Or, Moses bade eternal warfare wage
    With Amalek's ungracious progeny:
Or how the royal bard did groaning lie
    Beneath the stroke of Heaven's avenging ire;
Or Job's pathetic plaint, and wailing cry;
    Or rapt Isaiah's wild, seraphic fire;
Or other holy seers that tune the sacred lyre.

The Cotter's Saturday Night.

Perhaps the Christian volume is the theme,
How guiltless blood for guilty man was shed;
How HE, who bore in heaven the second name,
Had not on earth whereon to lay His head:
How His first followers and servants sped,
The precepts sage they wrote to many a land:
How he, who lone in Patmos banishèd,
Saw in the sun a mighty angel stand;
And heard great Bab'lon's doom pronounced by Heaven's command.

Then kneeling down, to HEAVEN'S ETERNAL KING,
The saint, the father, and the husband prays:
Hope "springs exulting on triumphant wing,"
That thus they all shall meet in future days:
There ever bask in uncreated rays,
No more to sigh or shed the bitter tear,
Together hymning their Creator's praise,
In such society, yet still more dear;
While circling time moves round in an eternal sphere.

Compared with this, how poor religion's pride,
In all the pomp of method, and of art,
When men display to congregations wide
Devotion's every grace, except the heart!
The Power, incensed, the pageant will desert,
The pompous strain, the sacerdotal stole:
But, haply, in some cottage far apart,
May hear, well pleased, the language of the soul;
And in His book of life the inmates poor enrol.

The Cotter's Saturday Night.

Then homeward all take off their several way;
   The youngling cottagers retire to rest:
The parent-pair their secret homage pay,
   And proffer up to Heaven the warm request
That HE, who stills the raven's clamorous nest,
   And decks the lily fair in flowery pride,
Would, in the way His wisdom sees the best,
   For them and for their little ones provide;
But, chiefly, in their hearts with grace divine preside.

From scenes like these old Scotia's grandeur springs,
   That makes her loved at home, revered abroad;
Princes and lords are but the breath of kings,
   "An honest man's the noblest work of GOD;"
And certes, in fair virtue's heavenly road,
   The cottage leaves the palace far behind.
What is a lordling's pomp?—a cumbrous load,
   Disguising oft the wretch of human kind,
Studied in arts of hell, in wickedness refined!

O Scotia! my dear, my native soil!
   For whom my warmest wish to Heaven is sent,
Long may thy hardy sons of rustic toil
   Be blest with health, and peace, and sweet content!
And, oh! may Heaven their simple lives prevent
   From luxury's contagion, weak and vile!
Then, howe'er crown and coronets be rent,
   A virtuous populace may rise the while,
And stand a wall of fire around their much-loved isle.

The Cotter's Saturday Night.

O Thou! who pour'd the patriotic tide
   ·That stream'd through Wallace's undaunted heart ;
Who dared to nobly ·stem tyrannic pride,
   Or nobly die, the second glorious part,
(The patriot's God, peculiarly Thou art,
   His friend, inspirer, guardian, and reward !)
Oh, never, never, Scotia's realm desert ;
   But still the patriot, and the patriot-bard,
In bright succession raise, her ornament and guard !

Halloween.[2]

---//---

Upon that night, when fairies light
  On Cassilis Downans dance,
Or owre the lays, in splendid blaze,
  On sprightly coursers prance;
Or for Colean the route is ta'en,
  Beneath the moon's pale beams;
There, up the cove, to stray and rove,
  Among the rocks and streams
          To sport that night.

Among the bonny winding banks
  Where Doon rins, wimplin', clear,
Where Bruce ance ruled the martial ranks,
  * And shook his Carrick spear,
Some merry, friendly, country-folks
  Together did convene,
To burn their nits, and pou their stocks,
  And haud their Halloween
          Fu' blithe that night.

Halloween.

The lasses feat, and cleanly neat,
  Mair braw than when they're fine;
Their faces blithe, fu' sweetly kythe,
  Hearts leal, and warm, and kin':
The lads sae' trig, wi' wooer-babs
  Weel knotted on their garten;
Some unco blate, and some wi' gabs
  Gar lasses' hearts gang startin'
        Whiles fast at night.

Then, first and foremost, through the kail,
  Their stocks maun a' be sought ance;
They steek their een, and graip and wale,
  For muckle anes and straught anes.
Poor hav'rel Will fell aff the drift,
  And wander'd through the bow-kail,
And pou't, for want o' better shift,
  A runt was like a sow-tail,
        Sae bow't that night.

Then, straught or crooked, yird or nane,
  They roar and cry a' throu'ther;
The very wee things, toddlin', rin,
  Wi' stocks out-owre their shouther;*
And gif the custoc's sweet or sour,
  Wi' joctelegs they taste them;
Syne cozily, aboon the door,
  Wi' cannie care, they've placed them
        To lie that night.

" *Whyles owre a linn the burnie plays,*
As through the glen it wimpl't;
Whyles round a rocky scaur it strays;
Whyles in a wiel it dimpl't;
Whyles glitter'd to the nightly rays,
Wi' bickering, dancing dazzle;
Whyles cookit underneath the braes,
Below the spreading hazel,
                Unseen that night."

Halloween.

The lasses staw frae 'mang them a'
  To pou their stalks o' corn :
But Rab slips out, and jinks about,
  Behint the muckle thorn :
He grippet Nelly hard and fast ;
  Loud skirl'd a' the lasses ;
But her tap-pickle maist was lost,
  When kitlin' in the fause-house
          Wi' him that night.

The auld guidwife's weel-hoordit nits
  Are round and round divided,
And mony lads' and lasses' fates
  Are there that night decided :
Some kindle coothie, side by side,
  And burn thegither trimly ;
Some start awa' wi' saucy pride,
  And jump out-owre the chimlie
          Fu' high that night.

Jean slips in twa wi' tentie ee ;
  Wha 'twas she wadna tell ;
But this is Jock, and this is me,
  She says in to hersel :
He bleezed owre her, and she owre him,
  As they wad ne'er mair part ;
Till, fuff! he started up the lum,
  And Jean had e'en a sair heart
          To see 't that night.

Halloween.

Poor Willie, wi' his bow-kail runt,
  Was brunt wi' primsie Mallie;
And Mallie, nae dout, took the drunt,
  To be compared to Willie;
Mall's nit lap out wi' pridefu' fling,
  And her ain fit it brunt it;
While Willie lap, and swore, by jing,
  'Twas just the way he wanted
         To be that night.

Nell had the fause-house in her min',
  She pits hersel and Rob in;
In loving bleeze they sweetly join,
  Till white in ase they're sobbin';
Nell's heart was dancin' at the view,
  She whisper'd Rob to leuk for't:
Rob, stowlins, prie'd her bonny mou',
  Fu' cozie in the neuk for't,
         Unseen that night.

But Merran sat behint their backs,
  Her thoughts on Andrew Bell;
She lea'es them gashin' at their cracks,
  And slips out by hersel:
She through the yard the nearest taks,
  And to the kiln she goes then,
And darklins graipit for the bauks,
  And in the blue-clue throws then,
         Right fear't that night.

Halloween.

And aye she win't, and aye she swat,
   I wat she made nae jaukin',
Till something held within the pat ;
   Guid Lord ! but she was quakin' !
But whether 'twas the deil himsel,
   Or whether 'twas a bauk-en',
Or whether it was Andrew Bell,
   She didna wait on talkin'
            To spier that night.

Wee Jenny to her grannie says,
   "Will ye go wi' me, grannie ?
I 'll eat the apple at the glass
   I gat frae Uncle Johnnie."
She fuff't her pipe wi' sic a lunt,
   In wrath she was sae vap'rin',
She notice't na, an aizle brunt
   Her braw new worset apron
            Out through that night.

"Ye little skelpie-limmer's face !
   I daur you try sic sportin',
As seek the foul thief ony place,
   For him to spae your fortune ;
Nae doubt but ye may get a sight !
   Great cause ye hae to fear it ;
For mony a ane has gotten a fright,
   And lived and died deleeret
            On sic a night.

Halloween.

"Ae hairst afore the Sherramoor,—
    I mind't as weel's yestreen,
I was a gilpey then, I'm sure
    I wasna past fifteen;
The simmer had been cauld and wat,
    And stuff was unco green;
And aye a rantin' kirn we gat,
    And just on Halloween
            It fell that night.

"Our stibble-rig was Rab M'Graen,
    A clever, sturdy fallow:
His son gat Eppie Sim wi' wean,
    That lived in Achmacalla:
He gat hemp-seed, I mind it weel,
    And he made unco light o't;
But mony a day was by himsel,
    He was sae sairly frighted
            That very night."

Then up gat fechtin' Jamie Fleck,
    And he swore by his conscience,
That he could saw hemp-seed a peck,
    For it was a' but nonsense.
The auld guidman raught down the pock,
    And out a handfu' gied him;
Syne bade him slip frae 'mang the folk,
    Some time when nae ane see'd him,
            And try't that night.

Halloween.

He marches through amang the stacks,
   Though he was something sturtin ;
The graip he for a harrow taks,
   And haurls it at his curpin ;
And every now and then he says,
   " Hemp-seed, I saw thee,
And her that is to be my lass,
   Come after me, and draw thee
           As fast this night."

He whistled up Lord Lennox' march
   To keep his courage cheery ;
Although his hair began to arch,
   He was sae fley'd and eerie :
Till presently he hears a squeak,
   And then a grane and gruntle ;
He by his shouther gae a keek,
   And tumbled wi' a wintle
           Out-owre that night.

He roar'd a horrid murder-shout,
   In dreadfu' desperation !
And young and auld cam rinnin' out
   To hear the sad narration :
He swore 'twas hilchin Jean M'Craw,
   Or crouchie Merran Humphie,
Till, stop ! she trotted through them a'—
   And wha was it but grumphie
           Asteer that night !

Halloween.

Meg fain wad to the barn hae gaen,
    To win three wechts o' naething;
But for to meet the deil her lane,
    She pat but little faith in:
She gies the herd a pickle nits,
    And twa red-cheekit apples,
To watch, while for the barn she sets,
    In hopes to see Tam Kipples
        That very night.

She turns the key wi' cannie thraw,
    And owre the threshold ventures;
But first on Sawnie gies a ca',
    Syne bauldly in she enters:
A ratton rattled up the wa',
    And she cried, Lord, preserve her!
And ran through midden-hole and a',
    And pray'd wi' zeal and fervour,
        Fu' fast that night.

They hoy't out Will, wi' sair advice;
    They hecht him some fine braw ane;
It chanced the stack he faddom't thrice,
    Was timmer-propt for thrawin';
He taks a swirlie, auld moss-oak,
    For some black, grousome carlin;
And loot a winze, and drew a stroke,
    Till skin in blypes cam haurlin'
        Aff's nieves that night.

Halloween.

A wanton widow Leezie was,
  As canty as a kittlin;
But, och! that night, amang the shaws,
  She got a fearfu' settlin'!
She through the whins, and by the cairn,
  And owre the hill gaed scrievin,
Whare three lairds' lands met at a burn,
  To dip her left sark-sleeve in,
          Was bent that night.

Whyles owre a linn the burnie plays,
  As through the glen it wimpl't;
Whyles round a rocky scaur it strays;
  Whyles in a wiel it dimpl't;
Whyles glitter'd to the nightly rays,
  Wi' bickering, dancing dazzle;
Whyles cookit underneath the braes,
  Below the spreading hazel,
          Unseen that night.

Amang the brackens, on the brae,
  Between her and the moon,
The deil, or else an outler quey,
  Gat up and gae a croon:
Poor Leezie's heart maist lap the hool!
  Near lav'rock-height she jumpit;
But mist a fit, and in the pool
  Out-owre the lugs she plumpit,
          Wi' a plunge that night.

Halloween.

In order, on the clean hearth-stane,
 The luggies three are ranged,
And every time great care is ta'en
 To see them duly changed :
Auld Uncle John, wha wedlock's joys
 Sin' Mar's year did desire,
Because he gat the toom dish thrice,
· He heaved them on the fire
                In wrath that night.

Wi' merry sangs, and friendly cracks,
 I wat they didna weary ;
And unco tales, and funny jokes,
 Their sports were cheap and cheery ;
Till butter'd so'ns, wi' fragrant lunt,
 Set a' their gabs a-steerin' ;
Syne, wi' a social glass o' strunt,
 They parted aff careerin'
                Fu' blythe that night.

A Winter Night.

———o———

When biting Boreas, fell and doure,
Sharp shivers through the leafless bower ;
When Phœbus gies a short-lived glower
        Far south the lift,
Dim-darkening through the flaky shower,
        Or. whirling drift :

Ae night the storm the steeples rocked,
Poor labour sweet in sleep was locked,
While burns, wi' snawy wreaths up-choked,
        Wild-eddying swirl,
Or through the mining outlet bocked,
        Down headlong hurl.

A Winter Night.

Listening the doors and winnocks rattle,
I thought me on the ourie cattle,
Or silly sheep, wha bide this brattle
      O' winter war,
And through the drift, deep-lairing sprattle,
      Beneath a scaur.

Ilk happing bird, wee, helpless thing,
That, in the merry months o' spring,
Delighted me to hear thee sing,
      What comes o' thee?
Whare wilt thou cower thy chittering wing,
      And close thy ee?

Even you, on murdering errands toil'd,
Lone from your savage homes exiled,
The blood-stain'd roost, and sheep-cot spoil'd,
      My heart forgets,
While pitiless the tempest wild
      Sore on you beats.

Now Phœbe, in her midnight reign,
Dark muffled, view'd the dreary plain;
Still crowding thoughts, a pensive train,
      Rose in my soul,
When on my ear this plaintive strain,
      Slow, solemn, stole :—

A Winter Night.

"Blow, blow, ye winds, with heavier gust!
And freeze, thou bitter-biting frost!
Descend, ye chilly, smothering snows!
Not all your rage, as now united, shows
  More hard unkindness, unrelenting,
  Vengeful malice unrepenting,
Than heaven-illumined man on brother man bestows!

  "See stern Oppression's iron grip,
    Or mad Ambition's gory hand,
  Sending, like blood-hounds from the slip,
    ·Woe, Want, and Murder o'er a land!
  Even in the peaceful rural vale,
  Truth, weeping, tells the mournful tale,
How pamper'd Luxury, Flattery by her side,
  The parasite empoisoning her ear,
  With all the servile wretches in the rear,
Looks o'er proud Property, extended wide;
  And eyes the simple rustic hind,
    Whose toil upholds the glittering show,
  A creature of another kind,
  Some coarser substance unrefined,
Placed for her lordly use thus far, thus vile, below.

  "Where, where is Love's fond, tender throe,
  With lordly Honour's lofty brow,

A Winter Night.

The powers you proudly own?
Is there, beneath Love's noble name,
Can harbour dark the selfish aim,
    To bless himself alone!
Mark maiden innocence a prey
    To love-pretending snares,
This boasted Honour turns away,
Shunning soft Pity's rising sway,
Regardless of the tears and unavailing prayers!
Perhaps this hour, in misery's squalid nest,
She strains your infant to her joyless breast,
And with a mother's fears shrinks at the rocking blast!

"O ye who, sunk in beds of down,
Feel not a want but what yourselves create,
Think for a moment on his wretched fate
    Whom friends and fortune quite disown!
Ill satisfied keen nature's clamorous call,
    Stretch'd on his straw he lays himself to sleep,
While through the ragged roof and chinky wall,
    Chill o'er his slumbers piles the drifty heap!
Think on the dungeon's grim confine,
Where Guilt and poor Misfortune pine!
    Guilt, erring man, relenting view!
    But shall thy legal rage pursue
    The wretch, already crushèd low
    By cruel Fortune's undeservèd blow?

A Winter Night.

Affliction's sons are brothers in distress ;
A brother to relieve, how exquisite the bliss !"

"*And hail'd the morning with a cheer,
A cottage-rousing craw.*"

I heard na mair, for chanticleer
   Shook off the pouthery snaw,
And hail'd the morning with a cheer,
   A cottage-rousing craw.

But deep this truth impress'd my mind—
   Through all His works abroad,
The heart benevolent and kind
   The most resembles God.

To a Mountain Daisy,

ON TURNING ONE DOWN WITH THE PLOUGH IN APRIL 1786.

————◊————

Wee, modest, crimson-tippèd flower,
Thou's met me in an evil hour;
For I maun crush amang the stoure
    Thy slender stem:
To spare thee now is past my power,
    Thou bonny gem.

Alas! it's no thy neibor sweet,
The bonny lark, companion meet,
Bending thee 'mang the dewy weet,
        Wi' speckled breast,
When upward springing, blithe, to greet,
        The purpling east.

Cauld blew the bitter-biting north
Upon thy early, humble birth;
Yet cheerfully thou glinted forth
        Amid the storm,
Scarce rear'd above the parent earth
        Thy tender form.

To a Mountain Daisy.

The flaunting flowers our gardens yield,
High sheltering woods and wa's maun shield;
But thou, beneath the random bield
    O' clod or stane,
Adorns the histie stibble-field,
    Unseen, alane.

There, in thy scanty mantle clad,
Thy snawie bosom sun-ward spread,
Thou lifts thy unassuming head
    In humble guise;
But now the *share* uptears thy bed,
    And low thou lies!

Such is the fate of artless maid,
Sweet floweret of the rural shade!
By love's simplicity betray'd,
    And guileless trust,
Till she, like thee, all soil'd, is laid
    Low i' the dust.

To a Mountain Daisy.

Such is the fate of simple bard,
On life's rough ocean luckless starr'd!
Unskilful he to note the card
              Of prudent lore,
Till billows rage, and gales blow hard,
              And whelm him o'er!

Such fate to suffering worth is given.
Who long with wants and woes has striven,
By human pride or cunning driven
              To misery's brink,
Till, wrench'd of every stay but Heaven,
              He, ruin'd, sink!

Even thou who mourn'st the Daisy's fate,
That fate is thine—no distant date;
Stern Ruin's ploughshare drives, elate,
              Full on thy bloom,
Till, crush'd beneath the furrow's weight,
              Shall be thy doom!

Address to Edinburgh.

———◊———

Edina! Scotia's darling seat!
   All hail thy palaces and towers,
Where once beneath a monarch's feet
   Sat Legislation's sovereign powers!
From marking wildly-scatter'd flowers,
   As on the banks of Ayr I stray'd,
And singing, lone, the lingering hours,
   I shelter in thy honour'd shade.

Here wealth still swells the golden tide,
   As busy Trade his labour plies;
There Architecture's noble pride
   Bids elegance and splendour rise:
Here Justice, from her native skies,
   High wields her balance and her rod;
There Learning, with his eagle eyes,
   Seeks Science in her coy abode.

Address to Edinburgh.

Thy sons, Edina! social, kind,
  With open arms the stranger hail;
Their views enlarged, their liberal mind
  Above the narrow, rural vale;
Attentive still to Sorrow's wail,
  Or modest Merit's silent claim;
And never may their sources fail!
  And never envy blot their name!

Thy daughters bright thy walks adorn,
  Gay as the gilded summer sky,
Sweet as the dewy milk-white thorn,
  Dear as the raptured thrill of joy!
Fair Burnet' strikes th' adoring eye,
  Heaven's beauties on my fancy shine;
I see the Sire of love on high,
  And own His works indeed divine.

There, watching high the least alarms,
  Thy rough, rude fortress gleams afar;
Like some bold veteran, gray in arms,
  And mark'd with many a seamy scar:
The ponderous wall and massy bar,
  Grim-rising o'er the rugged rock,
Have oft withstood assailing war,
  And oft repell'd the invader's shock.

"*There, watching high the least alarms,*
Thy rough, rude fortress gleams afar;
Like some bold veteran, gray in arms,
And mark'd with many a seamy scar.

Address to Edinburgh.

With awe-struck thought, and pitying tears,
   I view that noble, stately dome,
Where Scotia's kings of other years,
   Famed heroes! had their royal home:
Alas! how changed the times to come!
   Their royal name low in the dust!
Their hapless race wild-wandering roam!
   Though rigid law cries out, 'Twas just.

Wild beats my heart to trace your steps,
   Whose ancestors, in days of yore,
Through hostile ranks and ruin'd gaps
   Old Scotia's bloody lion bore : ～
Even I who sing in rustic lore,
   Haply, my sires have left their shed,
And faced grim Danger's loudest roar,
   Bold-following where your fathers led!

Edina! Scotia's darling seat!
   All hail thy palaces and towers,
Where once beneath a monarch's feet
   Sat Legislation's sovereign powers!
From marking wildly-scatter'd flowers,
   As on the banks of Ayr I stray'd,
And singing, lone, the lingering hours,
   I shelter in thy honour'd shade.

The Brigs of Ayr.

INSCRIBED TO JOHN BALLANTYNE, ESQ., AYR.

——o——

THE simple bard, rough at the rustic plough,
Learning his tuneful trade from every bough;
The chanting linnet, or the mellow thrush,
Hailing the setting sun, **sweet**, in the green-thorn bush;
The soaring lark, the perching redbreast shrill,
Or deep-toned plovers, gray, wild-whistling o'er the hill:
Shall he, nurst in the peasant's lowly shed,
To hardy independence bravely bred,
By early poverty to hardship steel'd,
And train'd to arms in stern Misfortune's field—
Shall he be guilty of their hireling crimes,
The servile, mercenary Swiss of rhymes?
Or labour hard the panegyric close,
With all the venal soul of dedicating prose?
No! though his artless strains he rudely sings,
And throws his hand uncouthly o'er the strings,
He glows with all the spirit of the bard,
Fame, honest fame, his great, his dear reward!
Still, if some patron's generous care he trace,
Skill'd in the secret, to bestow with grace;

The Brigs of Ayr.

When Ballantyne befriends his humble name,
And hands the rustic stranger up to fame,
With heart-felt throes his grateful bosom swells,
The godlike bliss, to give, alone excels.

'Twas when the stacks get on their winter-hap,
And thack and rape secure the toil-won crap;
Potato-bings are snuggèd up frae skaith
O' coming Winter's biting, frosty breath;

The bees, rejoicing o'er their summer toils,
Unnumber'd buds' and flowers' delicious spoils
Seal'd up with frugal care in massive waxen piles,
Are doom'd by man, that tyrant o'er the weak,
The death o' devils, smoor'd wi' brimstone reek:
The thundering guns are heard on every side;
The wounded coveys, reeling, scatter wide;
The feather'd field-mates, bound by Nature's tie,
Sires, mothers, children, in one carnage lie:

The Brigs of Ayr.

(What warm, poetic heart, but inly bleeds,
And execrates man's savage, ruthless deeds!)
Nae mair the flower in field or meadow springs,
Nae mair the grove with airy concert rings,
Except, perhaps, the robin's whistling glee,
Proud o' the height o' some bit half-lang tree:
The hoary morns precede the sunny days,
Mild, calm, serene, wide spreads the noontide blaze,
While thick the gossamer waves wanton in the rays.

'Twas in that season, when a simple bard,
Unknown and poor, simplicity's reward,
Ae night, within the ancient brugh of Ayr,
By whim inspired, or haply prest wi' care,
He left his bed, and took his wayward route,
And down by Simpson's wheel'd the left about:
(Whether impell'd by all-directing Fate,
To witness what I after shall narrate;
Or penitential pangs for former sins,
Led him to rove by quondam Merran Dins;
Or whether, rapt in meditation high,
He wander'd out, he knew not where nor why.)
The drowsy Dungeon clock had number'd two,
And Wallace Tower had sworn the fact was true:
The tide-swoln Firth, wi' sullen sounding roar,
Through the still night dash'd hoarse along the shore.

The Brigs of Ayr.

All else was hush'd as Nature's closèd ee:
The silent moon shone high o'er tower and tree:
The chilly frost, beneath the silver beam,
Crept, gently-crusting, o'er the glittering stream,

When, lo! on either hand the listening bard,
The clanging sugh of whistling wings is heard;
Two dusky forms dart through the midnight air,
Swift as the gos drives on the wheeling hare;
Ane on the Auld Brig his airy shape uprears,
The ither flutters o'er the rising piers:
Our warlock rhymer instantly descried
The sprites that owre the Brigs of Ayr preside.
(That bards are second-sighted is nae joke,
And ken the lingo of the spiritual folk;
Fays, spunkies, kelpies, a', they can explain them,
And even the very deils they brawly ken them.)
Auld Brig appear'd o' ancient Pictish race,
The very wrinkles Gothic in his face:
He seem'd as he wi' Time had warstled lang,
Yet, teughly doure, he bade an unco bang.
New Brig was buskit in a braw new coat,
That he at Lon'on frae ane Adams got;
In 's hand five taper staves as smooth 's a bead,
Wi' virls and whirlygigums at the head,
The Goth was stalking round with anxious search,
Spying the time-worn flaws in every arch ;—

The Brigs of Ayr.

It chanced his new-come neibor took his ee,
And e'en a vex'd and angry heart had he!
Wi' thieveless sneer to see his modish mien,
He, down the water, gies him this guid e'en :—

AULD BRIG.

I doubt na, frien', ye'll think ye're nae sheepshank,
Ance ye were streekit owre frae bank to bank!
But gin ye be a brig as auld as me—
Though, faith, that date I doubt ye'll never see—
There'll be, if that date come, I'll wad a boddle,
Some fewer whigmaleeries in your noddle.

NEW BRIG.

Auld Vandal, ye but show your little mense,
Just much about it, wi' your scanty sense;
Will your poor narrow footpath of a street—
Where twa wheelbarrows tremble when they meet—
Your ruin'd, formless bulk o' stane and lime,
Compare wi' bonny brigs o' modern time?
There's men o' taste would tak the Ducat Stream,
Though they should cast the very sark and swim,
Ere they would grate their feelings wi' the view
O' sic an ugly Gothic hulk as you.

The Brigs of Ayr.

AULD BRIG.

Conceited gowk! puff'd up wi' windy pride!
This mony a year I've stood the flood and tide;
And though wi' crazy eild I'm sair forfairn,
I'll be a brig when ye're a shapeless cairn!
As yet ye little ken about the matter,
But twa-three winters will inform ye better.
When heavy, dark, continued, a'-day rains,
Wi' deepening deluges o'erflow the plains;
When from the hills where springs the brawling Coil,
Or stately Lugar's mossy fountains boil,
Or where the Greenock winds his moorland course,
Or haunted Garpal draws his feeble source,
Aroused by blustering winds and spotting thowes,
In mony a torrent down his snaw-broo rowes;
While crashing ice, borne on the roaring spate,
Sweeps dams, and mills, and brigs, a' to the gate;
And from Glenbuck, down to the Ratton-key,
Auld Ayr is just one lengthen'd tumbling sea—
Then down ye'll hurl, deil nor ye never rise!
And dash the gumlie jaups up to the pouring skies.
A lesson sadly teaching, to your cost,
That Architecture's noble art is lost!

NEW BRIG.

Fine Architecture, trowth, I needs must say o't,
The Lord be thankit that we've tint the gate o't!

151

The Brigs of Ayr.

Gaunt, ghastly, ghaist-alluring edifices,
Hanging with threatening jut, like precipices;
O'erarching, mouldy, gloom-inspiring coves,
Supporting roofs fantastic, stony groves;
Windows and doors, in nameless sculpture drest,
With order, symmetry, or taste unblest;
Forms like some bedlam statuary's dream,
The crazed creations of misguided whim;
Forms might be worshipp'd on the bended knee,
And still the second dread command be free,
Their likeness is not found on earth, in air, or sea.
Mansions that would disgrace the building taste
Of any mason reptile, bird, or beast;
Fit only for a doited monkish race,
Or frosty maids forsworn the dear embrace;
Or cuifs of later times wha held the notion
That sullen gloom was sterling true devotion;
Fancies that our guid brugh denies protection!
And soon may they expire, unblest with resurrection! · -

AULD BRIG.

O ye, my dear-remember'd ancient yealings,
Were ye but here to share my wounded feelings!
Ye worthy proveses, and mony a bailie,
Wha in the paths o' righteousness did toil aye;
Ye dainty deacons, and ye douce conveeners,
To whom our moderns are but causey-cleaners!

152

The Brigs of Ayr.

Ye godly councils wha hae blest this town;
Ye godly brethren o' the sacred gown,
Wha meekly gae your hurdies to the smiters;
And (what would now be strange) ye godly writers;—
A' ye douce folk I've born aboon the broo,
Were ye but here, what would ye say or do!
How would your spirits groan in deep vexation
To see each melancholy alteration;
And, agonising, curse the time and place
When ye begat the base, degenerate race!
Nae langer reverend men, their country's glory,
In plain braid Scots hold forth a plain braid story!
Nae langer thrifty citizens and douce,
Meet owre a pint, or in the council-house;
But staumrel, corky-headed, graceless gentry,
The herryment and ruin of the country;
Men three parts made by tailors and by barbers,
Wha waste your weel-hain'd gear on damn'd new brigs
     and harbours!

NEW BRIG.

Now haud you there! for faith ye've said enough,
And muckle mair than ye can mak to through;
That's aye a string auld doited gray-beards harp on,
A topic for their peevishness to carp on.
As for your priesthood, I shall say but little,
Corbies and clergy are a shot right kittle:

The Brigs of Ayr.

But, under favour o' your langer beard,
Abuse o' magistrates might weel be spared :
To liken them to your auld-warld squad,
I must needs say comparisons are odd.
In Ayr, wag-wits nae mair can hae a handle
To mouth "a citizen," a term o' scandal ;
Nae mair the council waddles down the street,
In all the pomp of ignorant conceit ;
No difference but bulkiest or tallest,
With comfortable dulness in for ballast ;
Nor shoals nor currents need a pilot's caution,
For regularly slow, they only witness motion ;
Men wha grew wise priggin' owre hops and raisins,
Or gather'd liberal views in bonds and seisins ;
If haply Knowledge, on a random tramp,
Had shored them wi' a glimmer of his lamp,
And would to Common Sense for once betray'd them,
Plain, dull Stupidity stept kindly in to aid them.

———

What further clishmaclaver might been said,
What bloody wars, if sprites had blood to shed,
No man can tell ; but all before their sight,
A fairy train appear'd in order bright :
Adown the glittering stream they featly danced ;
Bright to the moon their various dresses glanced :
They footed o'er the watery glass so neat,   .
The infant ice scarce bent beneath their feet ;

The Brigs of Ayr.

While arts of minstrelsy among them rung,
And soul-ennobling bards heroic ditties sung.
Oh, had M'Lachlan, thairm-inspiring sage,
Been there to hear this heavenly band engage,
When through his dear strathspeys they bore with
    Highland rage ;
Or when they struck old Scotia's melting airs,
The lover's raptured joys or bleeding cares ;
How would his Highland lug been nobler fired,
And even his matchless hand with finer touch inspir'd !
No guess could tell what instrument appear'd,
But all the soul of Music's self was heard ;
Harmonious concert rung in every part,
While simple melody pour'd moving on the heart.

    The Genius of the stream in front appears,
A venerable chief advanced in years ;
His hoary head with water-lilies crown'd,
His manly leg with garter-tangle bound.
Next came the loveliest pair in all the ring, .
Sweet Female Beauty hand in hand with Spring ;
Then, crown'd with flowery hay, came Rural Joy,
And Summer, with his fervid-beaming eye :
All-cheering Plenty, with her flowing horn.
Led yellow Autumn, wreathed with nodding corn ;
Then Winter's time-bleach'd locks did hoary show,
By Hospitality with cloudless brow.

The Brigs of Ayr.

Next follow'd Courage, with his martial stride,
From where the Feal wild-woody coverts hide ;
Benevolence, with mild, benignant air,
A female form came from the towers of Stair :
Learning and Worth in equal measures trode
From simple Catrine, their long-loved abode :
Last, white-robed Peace, crowned with a hazel wreath,
To rustic Agriculture did bequeath
The broken iron instruments of death ;
At sight of whom our sprites forgat their kindling
    wrath.

Lines

WRITTEN WITH A PENCIL OVER THE CHIMNEYPIECE IN THE
PARLOUR OF THE INN AT KENMORE, TAYMOUTH.

———o———

ADMIRING Nature in her wildest grace,
These northern scenes with weary feet I trace;
O'er many a winding dale and painful steep,
The abodes of covey'd grouse and timid sheep,
My savage journey, curious, I pursue,
Till famed Breadalbane opens to my view,—
The meeting cliffs each deep-sunk glen divides,
The woods, wild scatter'd, clothe their ample sides,
The outstretching lake, embosom'd 'mong the hills,
The eye with wonder and amazement fills:
The Tay, meandering sweet in infant pride;
The palace, rising on its verdant side;
The lawns, wood-fringed in Nature's native taste;
The hillocks, dropt in Nature's careless haste;
The arches, striding o'er the new-born stream;
The village, glittering in the noontide beam—

    ❖   ❖   ❖   ✱

Poetic ardours in my bosom swell,
Lone wandering by the hermit's mossy cell:

Lines.

The sweeping theatre of hanging woods!
The incessant roar of headlong tumbling floods.

    ✦   ✦   ✦   ✦   ✦

Here Poesy might wake her Heaven-taught lyre,
And look through Nature with creative fire;
Here, to the wrongs of Fate half-reconciled,
Misfortune's lighten'd steps might wander wild;
And Disappointment, in these lonely bounds,
Find balm to soothe her bitter, rankling wounds;
Here heart-struck Grief might heavenward stretch
    her scan,
And injured Worth forget and pardon man.

    ✦   ✦   ✦

Verses

ON AN EVENING VIEW OF THE RUINS OF
LINCLUDEN ABBEY.

———o———

Ye holy walls, that, still sublime,
Resist the crumbling touch of time ;
How strongly still your form displays
The piety of ancient days!
As through your ruins, hoar and gray—
Ruins yet beauteous in decay—
The silvery moonbeams trembling fly,
The forms of ages long gone by
Crowd thick on Fancy's wondering eye,
And wake the soul to musings high.
Even now, as lost in thought profound,
I view the solemn scene around,
And, pensive, gaze with wistful eyes,
The past returns, the present flies ;
Again the dome, in pristine pride,
Lifts high its roof and arches wide,
That, knit with curious tracery,
Each Gothic ornament display.
The high-arch'd windows, painted fair,
Show many a saint and martyr there.

Lincluden Abbey.

As on their slender forms I gaze,
Methinks they brighten to a blaze!
With noiseless step and taper bright,
What are yon forms that meet my sight?
Slowly they move, while every eye
Is heavenward raised in ecstasy.
'Tis the fair, spotless, vestal train,
That seek in prayer the midnight fane.
And, hark! what more than mortal sound
Of music breathes the pile around?
'Tis the soft-chanted choral song,
Whose tones the echoing aisles prolong;
Till, thence return'd, they softly stray
O'er Cluden's wave, with fond delay;
Now on the rising gale swell high,
And now in fainting murmurs die.
The boatmen on Nith's gentle stream,
That glistens in the pale moonbeam,
Suspend their dashing oars to hear
The holy anthem, loud and clear;
Each worldly thought a while forbear,
And mutter forth a half-form'd prayer.
But, as I gaze, the vision fails,
Like frost-work touch'd by southern gales;
The altar sinks, the tapers fade,
And all the splendid scene's decay'd;
In window fair the painted pane
No longer glows with holy stain,

Lincluden Abbey.

But through the broken glass the gale
Blows chilly from the misty vale ;
The bird of eve flits sullen by,
Her home these aisles and arches high !
The choral hymn, that erst so clear
Broke softly sweet on Fancy's ear,
Is drown'd amid the mournful scream
That breaks the magic of my dream !
Roused by the sound, I start and see
The ruin'd sad reality !

Lament of Mary Queen of Scots on the Approach of Spring.

—— // ——

Now Nature hangs her mantle green
  On every blooming tree,
And spreads her sheets o' daisies white
  Out o'er the grassy lea:
Now Phœbus cheers the crystal streams,
  And glads the azure skies;
But nought can glad the weary wight
  That fast in durance lies.

Queen Mary's Lament.

Now lav'rocks wake the merry morn,
　Aloft on dewy wing;
The merle, in his noontide bower,
　Makes woodland echoes ring;
The mavis wild, wi' mony a note,
　Sings drowsy day to rest:
In love and freedom they rejoice,
　Wi' care nor thrall opprest.

Now blooms the lily by the bank,
　The primrose down the brae;
The hawthorn's budding in the glen,
　And milk-white is the slae;
The meanest hind in fair Scotland
　May rove their sweets amang;
But I, the queen of a' Scotland,
　Maun lie in prison strang!

I was the queen o' bonny France,
　Where happy I hae been;
Fu' lightly rase I in the morn,
　As blithe lay down at e'en:
And I'm the sov'reign of Scotland,
　And mony a traitor there;
Yet here I lie in foreign bands,
　And never-ending care.

Queen Mary's Lament.

But as for thee, thou false woman!
  My sister and my fae,
Grim Vengeance yet shall whet a sword
  That through thy soul shall gae!
The weeping blood in woman's breast
  Was never known to thee;
Nor the balm that draps on wounds of woe
  Frae woman's pitying ee.

My son! my son! may kinder stars
  Upon thy fortune shine!
And may those pleasures gild thy reign,
  That ne'er wad blink on mine!
God keep thee frae thy mother's faes,
  Or turn their hearts to thee:
And where thou meet'st thy mother's friend,
  Remember him for me!

Oh! soon to me may summer suns
  Nae mair light up the morn!
Nae mair to me the autumn winds
  Wave o'er the yellow corn!
And in the narrow house o' death
  Let winter round me rave;
And the next flowers that deck the spring
  Bloom on my peaceful grave!

" Now Nature hangs her mantle green
On every blooming tree."

Address to the Shade of Thomson,

ON CROWNING HIS BUST AT EDNAM, ROXBURGHSHIRE, WITH BAYS.

———o———

WHILE virgin Spring, by Eden's flood,
    Unfolds her tender mantle green,
Or pranks the sod in frolic mood,
    Or tunes Æolian strains between:

While Summer, with a matron grace,
    Retreats to Dryburgh's cooling shade,
Yet oft, delighted, stops to trace
    The progress of the spiky blade:

While Autumn, benefactor kind,
    By Tweed erects his agèd head,
And sees, with self-approving mind,
    Each creature on his bounty fed:

Address to the Shade of Thomson.

While maniac Winter rages o'er
  The hills whence classic Yarrow flows,
Rousing the turbid torrent's roar,
  Or sweeping, wild, a waste of snows ;—

So long, sweet Poet of the year!
  Shall bloom that wreath thou well hast won ;
While Scotia, with exulting tear,
  Proclaims that Thomson was her son !

Epistle to Davie,

A BROTHER POET.

———*o*———

WHILE winds frae aff Ben Lomond blaw,
And bar the doors wi' driving snaw,
   And hing us owre the ingle,
I set me down to pass the time,
And spin a verse or twa o' rhyme,
   In hamely westlin jingle.
While frosty winds blaw in the drift
   Ben to the chimla lug,
I grudge a wee the great folks' gift,
   That live sae bien and snug:
     I tent less, and want less
       Their roomy fire-side;
     But hanker and canker
       To see their cursèd pride.

Epistle to Davie.

It's hardly in a body's power
To keep at times frae being sour,
  To see how things are shared ;
How best o' chiels are whiles in want,
While coofs on countless thousands rant,
  And ken na how to wair't ;
But, Davie, lad, ne'er fash your head,
  Though we hae little gear,
We're fit to win our daily bread,
  As lang's we're hale and fier :
    "Mair spier na, nor fear na,"
      Auld age ne'er mind a feg ;
    The last o't, the warst o't,
      Is only but to beg.

To lie in kilns and barns at e'en,
When banes are crazed, and bluid is thin,
  Is doubtless great distress !
Yet then content could make us blest ;
E'en then, sometimes, we'd snatch a taste
  Of truest happiness.
The honest heart that's free frae a'
  Intended fraud or guile,
However Fortune kick the ba',
  Has aye some cause to smile :
    And mind still, you'll find still,
      A comfort this nae sma' ;
    Nae mair then, we'll care then,
      Nae farther can we fa'.

Epistle to Davie.

What though, like commoners of air,
We wander out we know not where,
 But either house or hall?
Yet nature's charms—the hills and woods,
The sweeping vales, and foaming floods—
 Are free alike to all.
In days when daisies deck the ground, -
 And blackbirds whistle clear,
With honest joy our hearts will bound
 To see the coming year :
  On braes, when we please, then,
   We'll sit and sowth a tune:
  Syne rhyme till't, we'll time till't,
   And sing't when we hae dune.

It"s no in titles nor in rank,
It's no in wealth like Lon'on bank,
 To purchase peace and rest :
It's no in making muckle mair ;
It's no in books ; it's no in lear ;
 To make us truly blest :
If happiness hae not her seat
 And centre in the breast,
We may be wise, or rich, or great,
 But never can be blest :
  Nae treasures, nor pleasures,
   Could make us happy lang :
  The heart aye's the part aye
   That makes us right or wrang.

Epistle to Davie.

Think ye that sic as you and I,
Wha drudge and drive through wet and dry,
  Wi' never-ceasing toil ;
Think ye, are we less blest than they
Wha scarcely tent us in their way,
  As hardly worth their while ?
Alas! how aft in haughty mood
  God's creatures they oppress !
Or else, neglecting a' that 's guid,
  They riot in excess !
    Baith careless and fearless
      Of either heaven or hell !
    Esteeming and deeming
      It 's ā' an idle tale !

Then let us cheerfu' acquiesce ;
Nor make our scanty pleasures less,
  By pining at our state ;
And, even should misfortunes come,
I here wha sit hae met wi' some,
  An 's thankfu' for them yet.
They gie the wit of age to youth ;
  They let us ken oursel ;
They make us see the naked truth,
  The real guid and ill.
    Though losses and crosses
      Be lessons right severe,
    There 's wit there, ye 'll get there,
      Ye 'll find nae other where.

Epistle to Davie.

But tent me, Davie, ace o' hearts!
(To say aught less wad wrang the cartes,
  And flattery I detest,)
This life has joys for you and I,
And joys that riches ne'er could buy,
  And joys the very best.
There's a' the pleasures o' the heart,
  The lover and the frien';
Ye hae your Meg, your dearest part,
  And I my darling Jean!
    It warms me, it charms me,
      To mention but her name:
    It heats me, it beets me,
      And sets me a' on flame!

Oh, all ye powers who rule above!
O Thou, whose very self art love!
  Thou know'st my words sincere!
The life-blood streaming through my heart,
Or my more dear immortal part,
  Is not more fondly dear!
When heart-corroding care and grief
  Deprive my soul of rest,
Her dear idea brings relief
  And solace to my breast.
    Thou Being, all-seeing,
      Oh, hear my fervent prayer!
    Still take her, and make her
      Thy most peculiar care!

Epistle to Davie.

All hail! ye tender feelings dear!
The smile of love, the friendly tear,
   The sympathetic glow!
Long since, this world's thorny ways
Had number'd out my weary days,
   Had it not been for you!
Fate still has blest me with a friend,
   In every care and ill;
And oft a more endearing band,
   A tie more tender still.
      It lightens, it brightens
         The tenebrific scene,
      To meet with, and greet with
         My Davie or my Jean!

Oh, how that name inspires my style!
The words come skelpin', rank and file,
   Amaist before I ken!
The ready measure rins as fine
As Phœbus and the famous Nine
   Were glowerin' owre my pen.
My spaviet Pegasus will limp,
   Till ance he's fairly het;
And then he'll hilch, and stilt, and jimp,
   And rin an unco fit:
      But lest then, the beast then,
         Should rue this hasty ride,
      I'll light now, and dight now
         His sweaty, wizen'd hide.

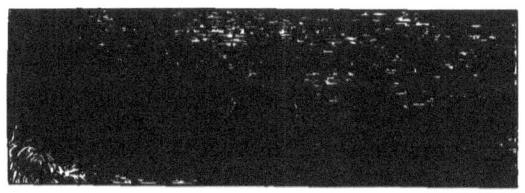

On Scaring some Water-Fowl in
Loch Turrit,

A WILD SCENE AMONG THE HILLS OF OCHTERTYRE.

———o———

Why, ye tenants of the lake,
For me your watery haunts forsake?
Tell me, fellow-creatures, why
At my presence thus you fly?
Why disturb your social joys,
Parent, filial, kindred ties?—
Common friend to you and me,
Nature's gifts to all are free:
Peaceful keep your dimpling wave,
Busy feed, or wanton lave;
Or, beneath the sheltering rock,
Bide the surging billow's shock.

On Scaring some Water-Fowl.

Conscious, blushing for our race,
Soon, too soon, your fears I trace.
Man, your proud usurping foe,
Would be Lord of all below :
Plumes himself in freedom's pride,
Tyrant stern to all beside.
The eagle, from the cliffy brow,
Marking you his prey below,
In his breast no pity dwells,
Strong necessity compels :
But man, to whom alone is given
A ray direct from pitying Heaven,
Glories in his heart humane—
And creatures for his pleasure slain.
In these savage, liquid plains,
Only known to wandering swains,
Where the mossy rivulet strays,
Far from human haunts and ways ;
All on nature you depend,
And life's poor season peaceful spend.
Or, if man's superior might
Dare invade your native right,
On the lofty ether borne,
Man with all his powers you scorn :
Swiftly seek, on clanging wings,
Other lakes and other springs ;
And the foe you cannot brave,
Scorn at least to be his slave.

"Prone down the rock the whitening sheet descends."

Lines

WRITTEN WITH A PENCIL, STANDING BY THE FALL OF FOYERS,
NEAR LOCH NESS.

———••———

AMONG the heathy hills and ragged woods
The roaring Foyers pours his mossy floods,
Till full he dashes on the rocky mounds,
Where, through a shapeless breach, his stream resounds.
As high in air the bursting torrents flow,
As deep-recoiling surges foam below,
Prone down the rock the whitening sheet descends,
And viewless Echo's ear, astonish'd, rends.
Dim seen through rising mists and ceaseless showers,
The hoary cavern, wide-surrounding, lowers.
Still, through the gap the struggling river toils,
And still, below, the horrid caldron boils.

   ✧   ✧   ✧   ✧   ✧

Epistle to a Young Friend.

———o———

I LANG hae thought, my youthfu' friend,
  A something to have sent you,
Though it should serve nae other end
  Than just a kind memento ;
But how the subject-theme may gang,
  Let time and chance determine ;
Perhaps it may turn out a sang,
  Perhaps turn out a sermon.

Ye'll try the world fu' soon, my lad ;
  And, Andrew, dear, believe me,
You'll find mankind an unco squad,
  And muckle they may grieve ye :
For care and trouble set your thought,
  Even when your end's attain'd ;
And a' your views may come to nought,
  Where every nerve is strain'd

Epistle to a Young Friend.

I 'll no say men are villains a' ;
  The real, harden'd, wicked,
Wha hae nae check but human law,
  Are to a few restricked :
But, och ! mankind are unco weak,
  And little to be trusted ;
If self the wavering balance shake,
  It 's rarely right adjusted !

Yet they wha fa' in fortune's strife,
  Their fate we shouldna censure,
For still the important end of life
  They equally may answer ;
A man may hae an honest heart,
  Though poortith hourly stare him ;
A man may tak a neibor's part,
  Yet hae na cash to spare him.

Aye free, aff han' your story tell,
  When wi' a bosom crony ;
But still keep something to yoursel
  Ye scarcely tell to ony.
Conceal yoursel as weel 's ye can
  Frae critical dissection ;
But keek through every other man,
  Wi' sharpen'd, sly inspection.

Epistle to a Young Friend.

The sacred lowe o' weel-placed love,
  Luxuriantly indulge it ;
But never tempt the illicit rove,
  Though naething should divulge it :
I waive the quantum o' the sin,
  The hazard of concealing ;
But, och ! it hardens a' within,
  And petrifies the feeling !

To catch Dame Fortune's golden smile,
  Assiduous wait upon her ;
And gather gear by every wile
  That's justified by honour ;
Not for to hide it in a hedge,
  Nor for a train-attendant,
But for the glorious privilege
  Of being independent.

The fear o' hell's a hangman's whip
  To haud the wretch in order ;
But where ye feel your honour grip,
  Let that aye be your border :
Its slightest touches, instant pause—
  Debar a' side pretences ;
And resolutely keep its laws,
  Uncaring consequences.

Epistle to a Young Friend.

The great Creator to revere
  Must sure become the creature ;
But still the preaching cant forbear,
  And even the rigid feature :
Yet ne'er with wits profane to range,
  Be complaisance extended ;
An atheist laugh's a poor exchange
  For Deity offended!

When ranting round in Pleasure's ring,
  Religion may be blinded ;
Or if she gie a random sting,
  It may be little minded ;
But when on life we're tempest-driven,
  A conscience but a canker,
A correspondence fix'd wi' Heaven
  Is sure a noble anchor!

Adieu, dear, amiable youth !
  Your heart can ne'er be wanting!
May prudence, fortitude, and truth
  Erect your brow undaunting !
In ploughman phrase, "God send you speed,"
  Still daily to grow wiser :
And may you better reck the rede
  Than ever did th' adviser!

To the Guidwife of Wauchope House.

——o——

GUIDWIFE,

I mind it weel, in early date,
When I was beardless, young, and blate,
And first could thrash the barn,
Or haud a yokin' at the pleugh;
And though forfoughten sair eneugh,
Yet unco proud to learn:
When first amang the yellow corn
A man I reckon'd was,
And wi' the lave ilk merry morn
Could rank my rig and lass,
Still shearing, and clearing,
The tither stookèd raw,
Wi' claivers and haivers
Wearing the day awa'.

To the Guidwife of Wauchope House.

Even then, a wish (I mind its power),
A wish that to my latest hour
  Shall strongly heave my breast—
That I, for poor auld Scotland's sake,
Some usefu' plan or beuk could make,
  Or sing a sang at least.
The rough burr-thistle, spreading wide
  Amang the bearded bear,
I turn'd the weeder-clips aside,
  And spared the symbol dear:
    No nation, no station,
      My envy e'er could raise;
    A Scot still, but blot still,
      I knew nae higher praise.

But still the elements o' sang,
In formless jumble, right and wrang,
  Wild floated in my brain;
Till on that hairst I said before,
My partner in the merry core,
  She roused the forming strain:
I see her yet, the sonsie quean,
  That lighted up my jingle,
Her witching smile, her pauky een,
  That gart my heart-strings tingle!
    I firèd, inspirèd,
      At every kindling keek,
    But bashing, and dashing,
      I fearèd aye to speak.

To the Guidwife of Wauchope House.

Health to the sex! ilk guid chiel says,
Wi' merry dance in winter-days,
  And we to share in common:
The gust o' joy, the balm o' woe,
The saul o' life, the heaven below,
  Is rapture-giving woman.
Ye surly sumphs, who hate the name,
  Be mindfu' o' your mither:
She, honest woman, may think shame
  That ye're connected with her.
    Ye're wae men, ye're nae men,
      That slight the lovely dears;
    To shame ye, disclaim ye,
      Ilk honest birkie swears.

For you, no bred to barn and byre,
Wha sweetly tune the Scottish lyre,
  Thanks to you for your line:
The marled plaid ye kindly spare,
By me should gratefully be ware;
  'Twad please me to the Nine.
I'd be mair vauntie o' my hap,
  Douce hingin' owre my curple,
Than ony ermine ever lap,
  Or proud imperial purple.
    Fareweel then, lang heal then,
      And plenty be your fa';
    May losses and crosses
      Ne'er at your hallan ca'!

My Nannie, O.

TUNE—" *My Nannie, O.*"

———o———

BEHIND yon hills, where Lugar flows
  'Mang moors and mosses many, O,
The wintry sun the day has closed,
  And I 'll awa' to Nannie, O.

The westlin wind blaws loud and shrill;
  The night's baith mirk and rainy, O;
But I 'll get my plaid, and out I 'll steal,
  And owre the hills to Nannie, O.

My Nannie's charming, sweet, and young,
  Nae artfu' wiles to win ye, O :
May ill befa' the flattering tongue
  That wad beguile my Nannie, O.

My Nannie, O.

Her face is fair, her heart is true,
　As spotless as she's bonny, O :
The opening gowan, wat wi' dew,
　Nae purer is than Nannie, O.

A country lad is my degree,
　And few there be that ken me, O ;
But what care I how few they be ?
　I 'm welcome aye to Nannie, O.

My riches a's my penny-fee,
　And I maun guide it cannie, O ;
But warl's gear ne'er troubles me,
　My thoughts are a' my Nannie, O.

Our auld guidman delights to view
　His sheep and kye thrive bonny, O ;
But I 'm as blithe that hauds his pleugh,
　And has na care but Nannie, O.

Come weel, come woe, I care na by,
　I 'll tak what Heaven will sen' me, O ;
Nae ither care in life have I
　But live and love my Nannie, O !

*" Flow gently, sweet Afton, among thy green braes,
Flow gently, sweet river, the theme of my lays."*

Afton Water.

TUNE—*" The Yellow-hair'd Laddie."*

———o———

FLOW gently, sweet Afton, among thy green braes,
Flow gently, I'll sing thee a song in thy praise;
My Mary's asleep by thy murmuring stream—
Flow gently, sweet Afton, disturb not her dream.

Thou stock-dove, whose echo resounds through the glen,
Ye wild whistling blackbirds in yon thorny den,
Thou green-crested lapwing, thy screaming forbear—
I charge you disturb not my slumbering fair.

Afton Water.

How lofty, sweet Afton, thy neighbouring hills,
Far mark'd with the courses of clear winding rills;
There daily I wander as noon rises high,
My flocks and my Mary's sweet cot in my eye.

How pleasant thy banks and green valleys below,
Where wild in the woodlands the primroses blow;
There, oft as mild evening weeps over the lea,
The sweet-scented birk shades my Mary and me.

Thy crystal stream, Afton, how lovely it glides,
And winds by the cot where my Mary resides;
How wanton thy waters her snowy feet lave,
As gathering sweet flowerets she stems thy clear wave.

Flow gently, sweet Afton, among thy green braes,
Flow gently, sweet river, the theme of my lays;
My Mary's asleep by thy murmuring stream—
Flow gently, sweet Afton, disturb not her dream!

The Braes o' Ballochmyle.

TUNE—"*Braes o' Ballochmyle.*"

——*o*——

THE Catrine woods were yellow seen,
  The flowers decay'd on Catrine lea,
Nae laverock sang on hillock green,
  But nature sicken'd on the ee.
Through faded groves Maria sang,
  Hersel' in beauty's bloom the while,
And aye the wild-wood echoes rang,
  Fareweel the Braes o' Ballochmyle!

Low in your wintry beds, ye flowers,
  Again ye'll flourish fresh and fair;
Ye birdies dumb, in withering bowers,
  Again ye'll charm the vocal air:
But here, alas! for me nae mair
  Shall birdie charm or floweret smile:
Fareweel the bonny banks of Ayr,
  Fareweel, fareweel, sweet Ballochmyle!

The Lass o' Ballochmyle.

TUNE—"*Miss Forbes's Farewell to Banff.*"

—*//*—

'Twas even—the dewy fields were green,
  On every blade the pearls hang,
The zephyrs wanton'd round the bean,
  And bore its fragrant sweets alang:
In every glen the mavis sang,
  All nature listening seem'd the while,
Except where greenwood echoes rang
  Amang the braes o' Ballochmyle.

With careless step I onward stray'd,
  My heart rejoiced in Nature's joy,
When musing in a lonely glade,
  A maiden fair I chanced to spy;
Her look was like the morning's eye,
  Her air like Nature's vernal smile;
Perfection whisper'd, passing by,
  Behold the lass o' Ballochmyle!

The Lass o' Ballochmyle.

Fair is the morn in flowery May,
  And sweet is night in autumn mild;
When roving through the garden gay,
  Or wandering in the lonely wild:
But woman, Nature's darling child!
  There all her charms she does compile;
Even there her other works are foil'd
  By the bonny lass o' Ballochmyle.

Oh! had she been a country maid,
  And I the happy country swain,
Though shelter'd in the lowest shed
  That ever rose on Scotland's plain :
Through weary winter's wind and rain,
  With joy, with rapture, I would toil;
And nightly to my bosom strain
  The bonny lass o' Ballochmyle!

Then pride might climb the slippery steep,
  Where fame and honours lofty shine;
And thirst of gold might tempt the deep,
  Or downward seek the Indian mine;
Give me the cot below the pine,
  To tend the flocks, or till the soil,
And every day have joys divine
  With the bonny lass o' Ballochmyle.

The Birks of Aberfeldy.

TUNE—" *The Birks of Aberfeldy.*"

——0——

Bonny lassie, will ye go,
Will ye go, will ye go;
Bonny lassie, will ye go
To the birks of Aberfeldy?

Now simmer blinks on flowery braes,
And o'er the crystal streamlet plays;
Come, let us spend the lightsome days
In the birks of Aberfeldy.

While o'er their heads the hazels hing,
The little birdies blithely sing,
Or lightly flit on wanton wing
In the birks of Aberfeldy.

The braes ascend, like lofty wa's,
The foaming stream deep-roaring fa's,
O'erhung wi' fragrant spreading shaws,
The birks of Aberfeldy.

The Birks of Aberfeldy.

The hoary cliffs are crown'd wi' flowers,
White o'er the linns the burnie pours,
And rising, weets wi' misty showers
 The birks of Aberfeldy.

Let Fortune's gifts at random flee,
They ne'er shall draw a wish frae me,
Supremely blest wi' love and thee,
 In the birks of Aberfeldy.

Blithe was She.

TUNE—"*Andrew and his Cutty Gun.*"

———0———

BLITHE, blithe, and merry was she,
Blithe was she butt and ben:
Blithe by the banks of Earn,
And blithe in Glenturit glen.

By Auchtertyre grows the aik,
  On Yarrow banks the birken shaw;
But Phemie was a bonnier lass
  Than braes o' Yarrow ever saw.

Her looks were like a flower in May,
  Her smile was like a simmer morn;
She trippèd by the banks of Earn,
  As light's a bird upon a thorn.

Blithe was She.

Her bonny face it was as meek
  As ony lamb upon a lea;
The evening sun was ne'er sae sweet
  As was the blink o' Phemie's ee.

The Highland hills I've wandered wide,
  And o'er the Lowlands I hae been;
But Phemie was the blithest lass
  That ever trod the dewy green.

The Banks of the Devon.

TUNE—"*Bhanarach dhoun a chruidh*."

——*n*——

How pleasant the banks of the clear, winding Devon,
   With green spreading bushes, and flowers blooming
      fair!
But the bonniest flower on the banks of the Devon
   Was once a sweet bud on the braes of the Ayr.

Mild be the sun on this sweet blushing flower,
   In the gay rosy morn, as it bathes in the dew!
And gentle the fall of the soft vernal shower,
   That steals on the evening each leaf to renew.

Oh, spare the dear blossom, ye orient breezes,
   With chill hoary wing, as ye usher the dawn!
And far be thou distant, thou reptile, that seizes
   The verdure and pride of the garden and lawn!

Let Bourbon exult in his gay gilded lilies,
   And England, triumphant, display her bright rose:
A fairer than either adorns the green valleys
   Where Devon, sweet Devon, meandering flows.

The Lazy Mist.

TUNE—"*Here's a health to my true love.*"

———0———

THE lazy mist hangs from the brow of the hill.
Concealing the course of the dark, winding rill!
How languid the scenes, late so sprightly, appear,
As Autumn to Winter resigns the pale year.

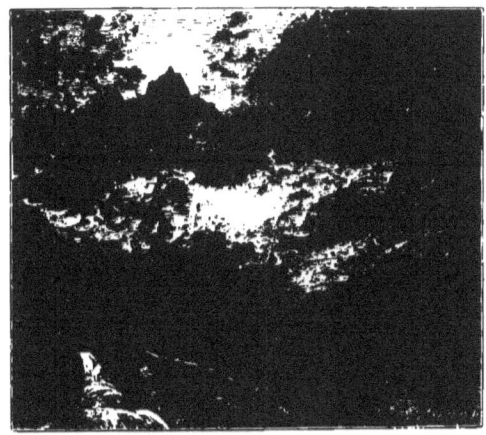

The forests are leafless, the meadows are brown,
And all the gay foppery of Summer is flown :
Apart let me wander, apart let me muse,
How quick Time is flying, how keen Fate pursues!

The Lazy Mist.

How long I have lived—but how much lived in
    vain!
How little of life's scanty span may remain!
What aspects old Time, in his progress, has worn!
What ties cruel Fate in my bosom has torn!
How foolish, or worse, till our summit is gain'd!
And downward, how weaken'd, how darken'd, how
    pain'd!
This life's not worth having, with all it can give—
For something beyond it poor man sure must live.

Of a' the Airts the Wind can Blaw.

TUNE—" *Miss Admiral Gordon's Strathspey.*"

——o——

OF a' the airts the wind can blaw,
  I dearly like the west,
For there the bonny lassie lives,
  The lassie I lo'e best :
There wild woods grow, and rivers row,
  And mony a hill between ;
But day and night, my fancy's flight
  Is ever wi' my Jean.

I see her in the dewy flowers,
  I see her sweet and fair ;
I hear her in the tunefu' birds,
  I hear her charm the air :
There's not a bonny flower that springs
  By fountain, shaw, or green,
There's not a bonny bird that sings,
  But minds me o' my Jean.

2 A

To Mary in Heaven.

TUNE—"*Death of Captain Cook.*"

—— o ——

Thou ling'ring star, with less'ning ray,
　That lov'st to greet the early morn,
Again thou usher'st in the day
　My Mary from my soul was torn.
O Mary! dear departed shade!
　Where is thy place of blissful rest?
See'st thou thy lover lowly laid?
　Hear'st thou the groans that rend his breast?

That sacred hour can I forget,
　Can I forget the hallow'd grove,
Where by the winding Ayr we met,
　To live one day of parting love!
Eternity will not efface
　Those records dear of transports past;
Thy image at our last embrace;
　Ah! little thought we 'twas our last!

To Mary in Heaven.

Ayr, gurgling, kiss'd his pebbled shore,
  O'erhung with wild woods, thick'ning green ;
The fragrant birch, and hawthorn hoar,
  Twined amorous round the raptured scene ;
The flowers sprang wanton to be prest,
  The birds sang love on every spray—
Till too, too soon, the glowing west
  Proclaim'd the speed of wingèd day.

Still o'er these scenes my memory wakes,
  And fondly broods with miser care !
Time but the impression stronger makes,
  As streams their channels deeper wear.
My Mary ! dear departed shade !
  Where is thy place of blissful rest ?
See'st thou thy lover lowly laid ?
  Hear'st thou the groans that rend his breast ?

Up in the Morning early.

The chorus of this song is old; but the two stanzas are Burns's.

———0———

CHORUS.

Up in the morning's no for me,
 Up in the morning early;
When a' the hills are cover'd wi' snaw,
 I'm sure it's winter fairly.

Cauld blaws the wind frae east to west,
 The drift is driving sairly;
Sae loud and shrill I hear the blast,
 I'm sure it's winter fairly.

The birds sit chittering in the thorn,
 A' day they fare but sparely;
And lang's the night frae e'en to morn,
 I'm sure it's winter fairly.

Musing on the Roaring Ocean.

TUNE—"*Druimion Dubh.*"

—o—

MUSING on the roaring ocean,
　Which divides my love and me;
Wearying Heaven in warm devotion,
　For his weal where'er he be.

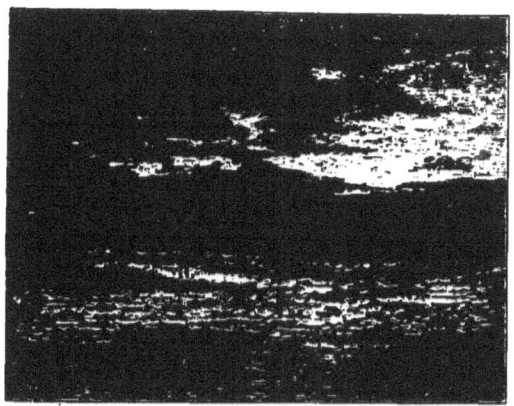

Hope and Fear's alternate billow
　Yielding late to Nature's law;
Whispering spirits round my pillow
　Talk of him that's far awa'!

Musing on the Roaring Ocean.

Ye whom sorrow never wounded,
　Ye who never shed a tear,
Care-untroubled, joy-surrounded,
　Gaudy Day to you is dear.

Gentle Night, do thou befriend me;
　Downy Sleep, the curtain draw;
Spirits kind, again attend me,—
　Talk of him that's far awa!

My Heart's in the Highlands.

TUNE—" Faille na Miosg."

—o—

My heart's in the Highlands, my heart is not here;
My heart's in the Highlands a-chasing the deer;
A-chasing the wild deer, and following the roe—
My heart's in the Highlands wherever I go.

Farewell to the Highlands, farewell to the North,
The birthplace of valour, the country of worth;
Wherever I wander, wherever I rove,
The hills of the Highlands for ever I love.

Farewell to the mountains high cover'd with snow;
Farewell to the straths and green valleys below;
Farewell to the forests and wild hanging woods;
Farewell to the torrents and loud-pouring floods.

My heart's in the Highlands, my heart is not here;
My heart's in the Highlands a-chasing the deer;
A-chasing the wild deer, and following the roe—
My heart's in the Highlands wherever I go.

The Banks of Nith.

TUNE—"*Robie donna Gorach.*"

—o—

THE Thames flows proudly to the sea,
  Where royal cities stately stand;
But sweeter flows the Nith to me,
  Where Cummins ance had high command:
When shall I see that honour'd land,
  That winding stream I love so dear!
Must wayward Fortune's adverse hand
  For ever, ever keep me here?

How lovely, Nith, thy fruitful vales,
  Where spreading hawthorns gaily bloom!
How sweetly wind thy sloping dales,
  Where lambkins wanton through the broom!
Though wandering, now, must be my doom,
  Far from thy bonny banks and braes,
May there my latest hours consume,
  Amang the friends of early days!

It is na, Jean, thy bonny face.

TUNE—"*The Maid's Complaint.*"

"These verses," says Cunningham, "were originally in English : Burns bestowed a Scottish dress upon them, and made them utter sentiments connected with his own affections."

———o———

It is na, Jean, thy bonny face
   Nor shape that I admire,
Although thy beauty and thy grace
   Might weel awake desire.
Something, in ilka part o' thee,
   To praise, to love, I find ;
But, dear as is thy form to me,
   Still dearer is thy mind.

Nae mair ungenerous wish I hae,
   Nor stronger in my breast,
Than if I canna mak thee sae,
   At least to see thee blest.
Content am I, if Heaven shall give
   But happiness to thee :
And as wi' thee I'd wish to live,
   For thee I'd bear to die.

Simmer's a pleasant Time.

TUNE—"*Aye Waukin, O.*"

——o——

SIMMER's a pleasant time,
　Flowers of every colour;
The water rins o'er the heugh,
　And I long for my true lover.

　　Aye waukin, O,
　　　Waukin still and wearie :
　　Sleep I can get nane
　　　For thinking on my dearie.

When I sleep I dream,
　When I wauk I'm eerie;
Sleep I can get nane
　For thinking on my dearie.

Lanely night comes on,
　A' the lave are sleepin';
I think on my bonny lad,
　And I blear my een w' greetin'.

Yon wild Mossy Mountains.

TUNE—"*Yon wild mossy Mountains.*"

——o——

"This song," says the poet, "alludes to a part of my private history which it is of no
consequence to the world to know."

Yon wild mossy mountains sae lofty and wide,
That nurse in their bosom the youth o' the Clyde,
Where the grouse lead their coveys through the heather
    to feed,
And the shepherd tends his flock as he pipes on his reed;
    Where the grouse lead their coveys through the heather
      to feed,
    And the shepherd tends his flock as he pipes on his reed.

Not Gowrie's rich valleys, nor Forth's sunny shores,
To me hae the charms o' yon wild mossy moors;
For there, by a lanely, sequester'd clear stream,
Resides a sweet lassie, my thought and my dream.
    For there, by a lanely, sequester'd clear stream,
    Resides a sweet lassie, my thought and my dream.

Yon wild Mossy Mountains.

Amáng thae wild mountains shall still be my path,
Ilk stream foaming down its ain green narrow strath;
For there, wi' my lassie, the day-lang I rove,
While o'er us, unheeded, flee the swift hours o'· love.

  For there, wi' my lassie, the day-lang I rove,
   While o'er us, unheeded, flee the swift hours o' love.

She is not the fairest, although she is fair;
O' nice education but sma' is her share;
Her parentage humble as humble can be;
But I lo'e the dear lassie because she lo'es me.

  Her parentage humble as humble can be,
  But I lo'e the dear lassie because she lo'es me.

To beauty what man but maun yield him a prize,
In her armour of glances, and blushes, and sighs?
And when wit and refinement hae polish'd her darts,
They dazzle our een as they flee to our hearts.

  And when wit and refinement hae polish'd her darts,
  They dazzle our een as they flee to our hearts.

But kindness, sweet kindness, in the fond sparkling ee,
Has lustre outshining the diamond to me;
And the heart-beating love, as I'm clasp'd in her arms,
Oh, these are my lassie's all-conquering charms!

  And the heart-beating love, as I'm clasp'd in her arms,
  Oh, these are my lassie's all-conquering charms!

"*Ca' them whare the heather grows.*"

Ca' the Yowes.

———◊———

Ca' the yowes to the knowes,
Ca' them whare the heather grows,
Ca' them whare the burnie rowes,
    My bonny dearie!

Hark the mavis' evening sang
Sounding Cluden's woods amang!
Then a-faulding let us gang,
    My bonny dearie.

Ca' the Yowes.

We'll gae down by Cluden side,
Through the hazels spreading wide,
O'er the waves that sweetly glide,
    To the moon sae clearly.

Yonder Cluden's silent towers,
Where at moonshine midnight hours,
O'er the dewy bending flowers,
    Fairies dance sae cheery.

Ghaist nor bogle shalt thou fear; ·
Thou'rt to love and heaven sae dear,
Nocht of ill may come thee near,
    My bonny dearie.

Fair and lovely as thou art,
Thou hast stown my very heart;
I can die—but canna part—
    My bonny dearie!

Countrie Lassie.

TUNE—"*The Country Lass.*"

—*o*—

IN simmer, when the hay was mawn,
  And corn waved green in ilka field,
While clover blooms white o'er the lea,
  And roses blaw in ilka bield;
Blithe Bessie in the milking shiel
  Says, "I'll be wed, come o't what will:"
Out spak a dame in wrinkled eild—
  "O' guid advisement comes nae ill.

"It's ye hae wooers mony ane,
  And, lassie, ye're but young, ye ken;
Then wait a wee, and cannie wale
  A routhie butt, a routhie ben:
There's Johnnie o' the Buskie Glen,
  Fu' is his barn, fu' is his byre;
Tak this frae me, my bonny hen,
  It's plenty beats the luver's fire."

Countrie Lassie.

" For Johnnie o' the Buskie Glen
    I dinna care a single flie;
He lo'es sae weel his craps and kye.
    He has nae luve to spare for me :
But blithe's the blink o' Robbie's ee,
    And weel I wat he loe's me dear :
Ae blink o' him I wadna gie
    For Buskie Glen and a' his gear."

" Oh, thoughtless lassie, life's a faught ;
    The canniest gate, the strife is sair,
But aye fu'-hant is fechtin' best—
    A hungry care's an unco care :
But some will spend, and some will spare,
    · And wilfu' folk maun hae their will ;
Syne as ye brew, my maiden fair,
    Keep mind that ye maun drink the yill."

" Oh, gear will buy me rigs o' land,
    And gear will buy me sheep and kye;
But the tender heart o' leesome luve
    The gowd and siller canna buy ;
We may be poor—Robbie and I,
    Light is the burden luve lays on ;
Content and luve bring peace and joy—
    What mair hae queens upon a throne ? "

My ain kind Dearie, O.

TUNE—" *The Lea Rig.*"

———o———

WHEN o'er the hill the eastern star
   Tells bughtin-time is near, my jo;
And owsen frae the furrow'd field
   Return sae dowf and weary, O;
Down by the burn, where scented birks
   Wi' dew are hanging clear, my jo,
I'll meet thee on the lea-rig,
   My ain kind dearie, O!

In mirkest glen, at midnight hour,
   I'd rove, and ne'er be eerie, O,
If through that glen I gaed to thee,
   My ain kind dearie, O!
Although the night were ne'er sae wild,
   And I were ne'er sae wearie, O,
I'd meet thee on the lea-rig,
   My ain kind dearie, O!

My ain kind Dearie, O.

The hunter lo'es the mornin' sun,
    To rouse the mountain deer, my jo;
At noon the fisher seeks the glen,
    Along the burn to steer, my jo;
Gie me the hour o' gloamin' gray,
    It maks my heart sae cheery, O,
To meet thee on the lea-rig,
    My ain kind dearie, O!

Highland Mary.

TUNE—"*Katharine Ogie.*"

—o—

Ye banks, and braes, and streams around
 The castle o' Montgomery,
Green be your woods, and fair your flowers,
 Your waters never drumlie!
There simmer first unfaulds her robes,
 And there the langest tarry;
For there I took the last fareweel
 O' my sweet Highland Mary.

How sweetly bloom'd the gay green birk!
 How rich the hawthorn's blossom!
As underneath their fragrant shade
 I clasp'd her to my bosom!
The golden hours, on angel wings,
 Flew o'er me and my dearie;
For dear to me, as light and life,
 Was my sweet Highland Mary!

Highland Mary.

Wi' mony a vow, and lock'd embrace,
  Our parting was fu' tender;
And, pledging aft to meet again,
  We tore oursels asunder;
But, oh! fell Death's untimely frost,
  That nipt my flower sae early!—
Now green's the sod, and cauld's the clay,
  That wraps my Highland Mary!

Oh, pale, pale now, those rosy lips,
  I aft hae kissed sae fondly!
And closed for aye the sparkling glance
  That dwelt on me sae kindly!
And mouldering now in silent dust
  That heart that lo'ed me dearly—
But still within my bosom's core
  Shall live my Highland Mary!

By Allan Stream I chanced to Rove.

TUNE—"*Allan Water.*"

—*o*——

By Allan stream I chanced to rove,
  While Phœbus sank beyond Benledi;
The winds were whispering through the grove,
  The yellow corn was waving ready:
I listen'd to a luver's sang,
  And thought on youthfu' pleasures many;
And aye the wild wood echoes rang—
  Oh, dearly do I love thee, Annie!

Oh, happy be the woodbine bower,
  Nae nightly bogle make it eerie;
Nor ever sorrow stain the hour,
  The place and time I met my dearie!
Her head upon my throbbing breast,
  She, sinking, said, "I'm thine for ever!"
While mony a kiss the seal imprest,
  The sacred vow,—we ne'er should sever.

By Allan Stream I chanced to Rove.

The haunt o' Spring's the primrose brae,
  The Simmer joys the flocks to follow;
How cheery, through her shortening day,
  Is Autumn in her weeds o' yellow!
But can they melt the glowing heart,
  Or chain the soul in speechless pleasure,
Or through each nerve the rapture dart,
  Like meeting her, our bosom's treasure?

"*Oft hae I rov'd by bonny Doon,*
To see the rose and woodbine twine;
And ilka bird sang o' its luve,
And fondly sae did I o' mine."

The Banks o' Doon.

TUNE.—"Caledonian Hunt's Delight."

YE banks and braes o' bonny Doon.
   How can ye bloom sae fresh and fair!
How can ye chant. ye little birds,
   And I sae weary. fu' o' care!

The Banks o' Doon.

Thou'lt break my heart, thou warbling bird,
　That wantons through the flowering thorn:
Thou minds me o' departed joys,
　Departed—never to return!

Oft hae I roved by bonny Doon,
　To see the rose and woodbine twine;
And ilka bird sang o' its luve,
　And fondly sae did I o' mine.
Wi' lightsome heart I pu'd a rose,
　Fu' sweet upon its thorny tree;
And my fause luver stole my rose,
　But, ah! he left the thorn wi' me.

Smiling Spring comes in rejoicing.

TUNE—" *The Bonny Bell.*"

————o————

THE smiling Spring comes in rejoicing,
   And surly Winter grimly flies;
Now crystal clear are the falling waters,
   And bonny blue are the sunny skies;
Fresh o'er the mountains breaks forth the morning,
   The evening gilds the ocean's swell;
All creatures joy in the sun's returning,
   .And I rejoice in my bonny Bell.

The flowery Spring leads sunny Summer,
   And yellow Autumn presses near,
Then in his turn comes gloomy Winter,
   Till smiling Spring again appear.
· Thus seasons dancing, life advancing,
   Old Time and Nature their changes tell,
But never ranging, still unchanging,
   . I adore my bonny Bell.

Coming through the Rye.

TUNE—"*Coming through the Rye.*"

———o———

COMING through the rye, poor body,
　　Coming through the rye,
She draiglet a' her petticoatie,
　　Coming through the rye.

　　O Jenny's a' wat, poor body,
　　　　Jenny's seldom dry;
　　She draiglet a' her petticoatie,
　　　　Coming through the rye.

Gin a body meet a body
　　Coming through the rye;
Gin a body kiss a body—
　　Need a body cry?

　　Gin a body meet a body
　　　　Coming through the glen;
　　Gin a body kiss a body—
　　　　Need the warld ken?

Is there for honest Poverty.

TUNE—"*For a' that, and a' that.*"

———o———

Is there for honest poverty,
  That hangs his head, and a' that?
The coward slave, we pass him by,
  We dare be poor for a' that!
For a' that, and a' that,
  Our toils obscure, and a' that;
The rank is but the guinea-stamp,
  The man's the gowd for a' that!

What though on hamely fare we dine,
  Wear hodden gray, and a' that;
Gie fools their silks, and knaves their wine,
  A man's a man for a' that!
For a' that, and a' that,
  Their tinsel show, and a' that;
The honest man, though e'er sae poor,
  Is king o' men for a' that!

Is there for honest Poverty.

Ye see yon birkie, ca'd a lord,
  Wha struts, and stares, and a' that;
Though hundreds worship at his word,
  He's but a coof for a' that:
For a' that, and a' that,
  His riband, star, and a' that;
The man of independent mind,
  He looks and laughs at a' that!

A king can mak a belted knight,
  A marquis, duke, and a' that;
But an honest man's aboon his might,
  Guid faith, he maunna fa' that!
For a' that, and a' that,
  Their dignities, and a' that;
The pith o' sense, and pride o' worth,
  Are higher ranks than a' that.

Then let us pray that come it may—
  As come it will for a' that—
That sense and worth, o'er a' the earth,
  May bear the gree, and a' that;
For a' that, and a' that,
  It's comin' yet for a' that,
That man to man, the warld o'er,
  Shall brothers be for a' that!

Caledonia.

TUNE—"*Humours of Glen.*"

——*o*——

THEIR groves o' sweet myrtle let foreign lands reckon,
  Where bright-beaming summers exalt their perfume;
Far dearer to me yon lone glen o' green breckan,
  Wi' the burn stealing under the lang yellow broom:

Far dearer to me are yon humble broom bowers,
  Where the blue-bell and gowan lurk lowly unseen;
For there, lightly tripping amang the wild flowers,
  A-listening the linnet, aft wanders my Jean.

Though rich is the breeze in their gay sunny valleys,
  And cauld Caledonia's blast on the wave;
Their sweet-scented woodlands that skirt the proud palace,
  What are they?—The haunt o' the tyrant and slave!

The slave's spicy forests, and gold-bubbling fountains,
  The brave Caledonian views wi' disdain;
He wanders as free as the winds of his mountains,
  Save Love's willing fetters—the chains o' his Jean.

Oh, wert thou in the Cauld Blast.

—o—

Oh, wert thou in the cauld blast
　On yonder lea, on yonder lea,
My plaidie to the angry airt,
　I'd shelter thee, I'd shelter thee:
Or did Misfortune's bitter storms
　Around thee blaw, around thee blaw,
Thy bield should be my bosom,
　To share it a', to share it a'.

Or were I in the wildest waste,
　Sae bleak and bare, sae bleak and bare,
The desert were a paradise,
　If thou wert there, if thou wert there:
Or were I monarch o' the globe,
　Wi' thee to reign, wi' thee to reign,
The brightest jewel in my crown
　Wad be my queen, wad be my queen.

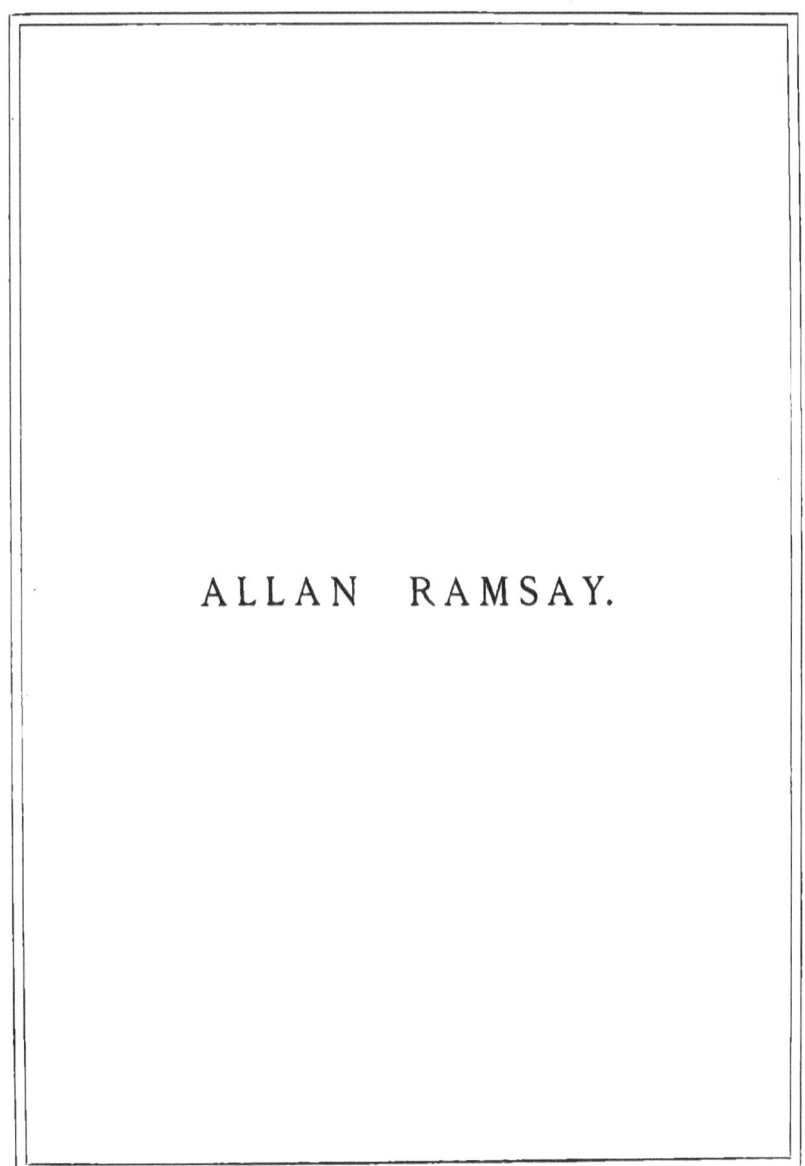

ALLAN RAMSAY.

Dialogue on Marriage.

——*o*——

PEGGY AND JENNY.

A flowery howm, between twa verdant braes,
Where lasses used to wash and spread their claes,
A trottin' burnie whimpling through the ground,
Its channel peebles, shining, smooth and round :
Here view twa barefoot beauties, clean and clear ;
First please your eye, then gratify your ear :
While Jenny what she wishes discommends,
And Meg, wi' better sense, true love defends.

Jenny. Come, Meg, let's fa' to wark upon this green,
This shining day will bleach our linen clean ;
The water clear, the lift's unclouded blue,
Will mak them like a lily wet wi' dew.

Peggy. Gae farer up the burn to Habbie's How,
Where a' the sweets o' spring an' simmer grow ;
Between twa birks, out o'er a little linn,
The water fa's and maks a singin' din :
A pool breast-deep beneath as clear as glass,
Kisses with easy whirls the bord'ring grass.
We'll end our washing while the morning's cool,
And when the day grows het, we'll to the pool ;
There wash oursels—'tis healthfu' now in May,
And sweetly cauler on sae warm a day.

Dialogue on Marriage.

Jenny. Daft lassie, when we're naked, what'll ye say
Gif our twa herds come brattling down the brae,
And see us sae? that jeering fallow Pate,
Wad taunting say, Haith, lasses, ye're no blate!

Peggy. We're far frae ony road, and out o' sight;
The lads they're feeding far beyont the height.
But tell me now, dear Jenny (we're our lane),
What gars ye plague your wooer wi' disdain?
The neibours a' tent this as weel as I,
That Roger loes ye, yet ye carena by.
What ails ye at him? Troth, between us twa,
He's wordy you the best day e'er ye saw.

Jenny. I dinna like him, Peggy, there's an end;
A herd mair sheepish yet I never kend.
He kaims his hair, indeed, and gaes right snug,
Wi' ribbon knots at his blue bonnet lug,
Whilk pensylie he wears a thought a-jee,
And spreads his gartens diced beneath his knee:
He faulds his o'erlay down his breast wi' care,
And few gang trigger to the kirk or fair:
For a' that, he can neither sing nor say,
Except " How d'ye?"—or, " There's a bonny day."

Peggy. Ye dash the lad wi' constant slighting pride,
Hatred for love is unco sair to bide;
But ye'll repent ye, if his love grow cauld:
What like's a dorty maiden when she's auld?

" *Gae farer up the burn to Habbie's How,*
Where a' the sweets o' Spring and Simmer grow;
Between twa birks, out o'er a little lin,
The water fa's and maks a singin' din."

Dialogue on Marriage.

Like dawted wean, that tarrows at his meat,
That for some feckless whim will orp and greet :
The lave laugh at it, till the dinner's past ;
And syne the fool thing is obliged to fast,
Or scart anither's leavings at the last.

Jenny.   Hey, " Bonny lass o' Branksome ! " ort' be lang
Your witty Pate will put you in a sang.
O 'tis a pleasant thing to be a bride,
Syne whinging gets about your ingle-side,
Yelping for this or that wi' fashous din ;
To mak them brats then ye maun toil and spin.
Ae wean fa's sick, an' scads itsel wi' broe,
Ane breaks his shin, another tines his shoe ;
The " Deil gaes o'er Jock Wabster," hame grows hell,
And Pate misca's ye waur than tongue can tell.

Peggy.   Yes, it's a heartsome thing to be a wife,
When round the ingle-edge young sprouts are rife.
Gif I'm sae happy, I shall hae delight
To hear their little plaints, an' keep them right.
Wow ! Jenny, can there greater pleasure be,
Than see sic wee tots toolying at your knee ;
When a' they ettle at——their greatest wish
Is to be made o', and obtain a kiss ?
Can there be toil in tenting day and night
The like o' them, when love maks care delight ?

Dialogue on Marriage.

Jenny. But poortith, Peggy, is the warst of a',
Gif o'er your heads ill-chance should begg'ry draw,
But little love or canty cheer can come
Frae duddy doublets, and a pantry toom.
Your nowt may die ;—the spate may bear away
Frae aff the howms your dainty rucks o' hay.
The thick-blawn wreaths o' snaw, or blashy thows,
May smoor your wathers, and may rot your ewes.
A dyvour buys your butter, woo, and cheese,
But, or the day o' payment, breaks, and flees :
Wi' gloomin' brow, the laird seeks in his rent;
It's no to gie ; your merchant's to the bent :
His honour mauna want ; he poinds your gear :
Syne, driven frae house an hald, where will ye steer ?
Dear Meg, be wise, and live a single life ;
Troth, it's nae mows to be a married wife.

Peggy. May sic ill luck befa' that silly she
Wha has sic fears, for that was never me.
Let fouk bode weel, an' strive to do their best :
Nae mair's required ; let Heav'n mak out the rest.
I've heard my honest uncle aften say,
That lads should a' for wives that's virtuous pray :
For the maist thrifty man could never get
A weel-stored room, unless his wife wad let :
Wherefore nocht shall be wanting on my part,
To gather wealth to raise my shepherd's heart;
Whate'er he wins, I'll guide wi' canny care,

Dialogue on Marriage.

And win the vogue at market, tron, or fair,
For halesome, clean, cheap, and sufficient ware.
A flock o' lambs, cheese, butter, and some woo,
Shall first be sauld, to pay the laird his due ;
Syne a' behind's our ain.————Thus, without fear,
Wi' love an' routh, we through the warld will steer :
And when my Pate in bairns and gear grows rife,
He'll bless the day he gat me for his wife.

Jenny. But what if some young giglet on the green,
Wi' dimpled cheeks an' twa bewitching een,
Shou'd gar your Patie think his half-worn Meg,
And her kenn'd kisses, hardly worth a feg ?

Peggy. Nae mair o' that—Dear Jenny, to be free,
There's some men constanter in love than we :
Nor is the ferly great, when Nature kind
Has blest them wi' solidity of mind.
They'll reason calmly, and wi' kindness smile,
When our short passions wad our peace beguile ;
Sae, whensoe'er they slight their maiks at hame,
It's ten to ane the wives are maist to blame.
Then I'll employ wi' pleasure a' my art
To keep him cheerfu', and secure his heart.
At e'en, when he comes weary frae the hill,
I'll hae a' things made ready to his will.
In winter, when he toils thro' wind and rain,
A bleezing ingle and a clean hearth-stane ;

Dialogue on Marriage.

An' soon as he flings by his plaid an' staff,
The seething pat's be ready to tak aff;
Clean hag-a-bag I'll spread upon his board,
And serve him wi' the best we can afford;
Good humour and white bigonets shall be
Guards to my face, to keep his love for me.

   Jenny. A dish o' married love right soon grows cauld,
An' dosens down to nane, as fouk grow auld.

   Peggy. But we'll grow auld thegither, and ne'er find
The loss o' youth, when love grows on the mind.
Bairns and their bairns mak sure a firmer tie,
Than ought in love the like of us can spy.
See yon twa elms that grow up side by side,
Suppose them some years syne bridegroom and bride;
Nearer and nearer ilka year they've prest,
Till wide their spreading branches are increas'd,
And in their mixture now are fully blest:
This shields the other frae the eastlin blast,
That, in return, defends it frae the wast.
Sic as stand single (a state sae liked by you!)
Beneath ilk storm, frae every airt, maun bow.

   Jenny. I've done—I yield, dear lassie, I maun yield;
Your better sense has fairly won the field,
With the assistance of a little fae
Lies darn'd within my breast this mony a day.

                         —The Gentle Shepherd.

NOTES.

NOTE 1.— *The Cotter's Saturday Night.* Page 113.

GILBERT BURNS gives the following distinct account of the origin of this poem :—
"Robert had frequently remarked to me that he thought there was something peculiarly venerable in the phrase, 'Let us worship God!' used by a decent, sober head of a family, introducing family-worship. To this sentiment of the author the world is indebted for 'The Cotter's Saturday Night.' When Robert had not some pleasure in view in which I was not thought fit to participate, we used frequently to walk together, when the weather was favourable, on the Sunday afternoons, those precious breathing-times to the labouring part of the community, and enjoyed such Sundays as would make one regret to see their number abridged. It was in one of these walks that I first had the pleasure of hearing the author repeat 'The Cotter's Saturday Night.' I do not recollect to have read or heard anything by which I was more highly electrified. The fifth and sixth stanzas, and the eighteenth, thrilled with peculiar ecstasy through my soul. The cotter, in the 'Saturday Night,' is an exact copy of my father in his manners, his family devotion, and exhortations ; yet the other parts of the description do not apply to our family. None of us were 'at service out among the farmers roun'.' Instead of our depositing our 'sair-won penny-fee' with our parents, my father laboured hard, and lived with the most rigid economy, that he might be able to keep his children at home, thereby having an opportunity of watching the progress of our young minds, and forming in them early habits of piety and virtue ; and from this motive alone did he engage in farming, the source of all his difficulties and distresses."

NOTE 2,— *Halloween.* Page 121.

The first ceremony of Halloween is pulling each a stock or plant of kail. They must go out, hand-in-hand, with eyes shut, and pull the first they meet with ; its being big or little, straight or crooked, is prophetic of the size and shape of the grand object of all their spells—the husband or wife. If any yird, or earth, stick to the root, that is tochur, or fortune, and the taste of the custoc—that is, the heart of the stem—is indicative of the natural temper and disposition. Lastly, the stems, or, to give them their ordinary appellation, the runts, are placed somewhere above the head of the door ; and the Christian names of the people whom chance brings into the house, are, according to the priority of placing the runts, the names in question.— *B.*

Page 125.

They go to the barn-yard and pull each, at three several times, a stalk of oats. If the third stalk wants the top pickle—that is, the grain at the top of the stalk—the party in question will come to the marriage-bed anything but a maid.— *B.*

When the corn is in a doubtful state, by being too green or wet, the stack-builder, by means of old timber, etc., makes a large apartment in his stack, with an opening in the side which is fairest exposed to the wind : this he calls a fause-house.— *B.*

Burning the nuts is a famous charm. They name the lad and lass to each particular nut as they lay them in the fire, and accordingly as they burn quietly together, or start from beside one another, the course and issue of the courtship will be.— *B.*

Page 126.

Whoever would, with success, try this spell, must strictly observe these directions :—Steal out, all alone, to the kiln, and darkling throw into the pot a clue of blue yarn ; wind it in a new clue of the old one ; and, towards the latter end, something will hold the thread ; demand "Wha hauds?"—*i.e.* who holds? An answer will be returned from the kiln-pot, by naming the Christian and surname of your future spouse.— *B.*

Page 127.

Take a candle, and go alone to a looking-glass ; eat an apple before it, and some traditions say you should comb your hair all the time ; the face of your conjugal companion *to be*, will be seen in the glass, as if peeping over your shoulder.— *B.*

Page 129.

Steal out unperceived, and sow a handful of hemp-seed, harrowing it with anything you can conveniently draw after you. Repeat now and then, "Hemp-seed, I saw thee ; hemp-seed, I saw thee ; and her (or him) that is to be my true love, come after me and pou thee." Look over your left shoulder, and you will see the appearance of the person invoked, in the attitude of pulling hemp. Some traditions say, "Come after me and shaw thee," that is, show thyself ; in which case it simply appears. Others omit the harrowing, and say, "Come after me and harrow thee."—*B.*

Page 130.

This charm must likewise be performed unperceived and alone. You go to the barn, and open both doors, taking them off the hinges, if possible, for there is danger that the being about to appear may shut the doors, and do you some mischief. Then take that instrument used in winnowing the corn, which in our country dialect we call a wecht ; and go through all the attitudes of letting down corn against the wind. Repeat it three times ; and the third time an apparition will pass through the barn, in at the windy door, and out at the other, having both the figure in question and the appearance of retinue marking the employment or station in life.— *B.*

Take an opportunity of going unnoticed to a bean-stack, and fathom it three times round. The last fathom of the last time you will catch in your arms the appearance of your future conjugal yoke-fellow.— *B.*

Page 131.

You go out, one or more, for this is a social spell, to a south-running spring or rivulet, where "three lairds' lands meet," and dip your left shirt-sleeve. Go to bed in sight of a fire, and hang your wet sleeve before it to dry. Lie awake ; and sometime near midnight an apparition having the exact figure of the grand object in question will come and turn the sleeve, as if to dry the other side of it.— *B.*

Page 132.

Take three dishes ; put clean water in one, foul water in another, leave the third empty : blindfold a person, and lead him to the hearth where the dishes are ranged ; he (or she) dips the left hand ; if by chance in the clean water, the future husband or wife will come to the bar of matrimony a maid ; if in the foul, a widow ; if in the empty dish, it foretells, with equal certainty, no marriage at all. It is repeated three times, and every time the arrangement of the dishes is altered.— *B.*

GLOSSARY.

www.ingramcontent.com/pod-product-compliance
Lightning Source LLC
Chambersburg PA
CBHW030803020726
47499CB00006B/1750